Erotom

CW01499173

Jon Athan

For more information on this book or the author,
please visit www.jon-athan.com. General
inquiries are welcome.

Facebook:
https://www.facebook.com/AuthorJonAthan
Twitter: @Jonny_Athan
Email: info@jon-athan.com

Book cover by Paramita:
http://www.creativeparamita.com/

Thank you for the support!

ISBN: 9781089794844

First Edition

WARNING

This book contains scenes of intense violence and some disturbing themes. Some parts of this book may be considered violent, cruel, disturbing, or unusual. Certain implications may also trigger strong emotional responses. This book is also *not* intended for those easily offended or appalled. Please enjoy at your own discretion.

Table of Contents

Chapter One

Pillow Talk

The floorboards creaked, the sheets rustled, and the headboard thumped on the wall. A man grunted and groaned, a woman moaned and giggled. The sound of love echoed through the small home—a loud but tender symphony of sex.

Ethan Miller lay atop his date in the missionary position, his body wavering like a snake as he thrust into her. Beads of sweat glistened across his muscular figure and dripped from his scruffy hair. His heart pounded in his chest, accelerating with each thrust. He could feel a warm sensation in his body—*was it love?*

Veins bulging on his neck and brow, Ethan said, "I'm... *cumming.*" He loudly exhaled and grunted as he ejaculated in his date. As he caught his breath, he whispered, "Shit, I thought I would have lasted longer by now..."

He dismounted and fell to his side. He rested on his back and wiped the sweat from his lean body. He vacantly stared at the ceiling as he thought about the sex: *did I pleasure her? Was I premature?* Those questions—those *damn* questions—always tormented him after sex. He glanced over at his date and smiled nervously.

Karen Wright, his girlfriend, stared back at him. The woman was a bit older than Ethan—she was pushing thirty. Her long black hair was sprawled across her pillow. She didn't cover herself up, so her perky breasts and freshly shaved crotch were displayed for the world to see. She didn't mind, either. She felt comfortable around her boyfriend.

Karen said, "You were good, Ethan." Those words made Ethan grin from ear-to-ear. The woman continued, "I mean, if it makes you feel better, you lasted longer than most men I've been with. Not bad for a 25-year-old."

"Twenty-four."

"What?"

"Twenty-four. I'm 24 years old."

Karen nodded and said, "Yeah, you're right. It's not a big difference, though. You were better than, you know, people in their twenties. That range or whatever..."

Ethan turned his attention to the ceiling. The shit-eating grin slowly vanished from his face. The warmth he felt in his body during sex was gone, replaced with a chilly sensation. Relationships were built on trust, loyalty, and respect—and that caused problems for Ethan.

Karen was not pleasured during sex. She was lying to him, he could not trust her. The woman candidly spoke about her past sexual relationships, which made Ethan feel like she was not pure—like she was not loyal.

And, worst of all, she forgot his birthday. What kind of person forgets their lover's birthday? A respectful person would never do such a thing.

Karen tapped Ethan's shoulder and asked, "Are you okay, hun?"

"I'm... I'm fine. I'm just thinking."

Indeed, Ethan was thinking—he wouldn't lie to his

lover. The man was trapped in a torrent of disappointing thoughts. He didn't feel any magic while having sex with Karen. He didn't feel any love or passion after their sex. Sex without love was nothing to him.

As Ethan brooded, Karen said, "I don't want you to feel bad, Ethan. I'm serious: it was good. You know, maybe we can try some foreplay next time. That way, you know, you wouldn't feel insecure or anything like that after. It's not like it's hard or anything. You just..."

Ethan looked away and grimaced, frustrated. He couldn't bear to listen to Karen's sexual advice. He stared down at himself, disappointed. He stared past his bulging chest and well-defined abs. In terms of muscle, he overcompensated for his other shortcomings. He wasn't worried about his physique, though.

He focused on his crotch.

His penis was ten centimeters erect—about four inches. At best, he could pass for eleven centimeters with a good camera angle. To his dismay, his penis appeared to be shrinking before his very eyes. It shrank to the size of a shriveled grape. He could barely see it through his pubic hair.

Teary-eyed, Ethan looked away and tried to stop himself from crying. He could feel vibrations in his ears—annoying thrumming, as if a fly were purposely pestering him by flying around his ears. *I was wrong,* he thought, *she's not the one for me.*

As she glanced around the room, Karen said, "I think this is the first time I've ever looked around your room. Usually, you come to my place or we... we do a quickie, then I leave. It's... It's cool in here. You have a lot of movie posters on your walls." She sat up and examined the desk across the room. She said, "You have a lot of movies and books, too. Are they all about horror stuff?"

Trying to keep his composure, Ethan glanced around his room. Framed movie posters hung on the walls to his left and right—*Aliens, The Thing, The Texas Chainsaw Massacre,* and the gist. A stack of Blu-ray movies sat on his desk next to his computer. Horror novels sat on a shelf above the desk, too. He loved horror.

In a cracking voice, Ethan said, "Yeah. They... They're horror movies and novels. They're my... my favorites. I have more in the closet."

"Cool. I like horror movies, too. I haven't watched any of these, though. I usually watch, like, ghost movies and stuff. Maybe we can watch one later?"

"Sure, sure..."

Karen squirmed closer to her boyfriend, then she placed her head on his firm chest. She said, "I know we've been dating for a while, but I still don't know what you do. You said you worked independently, right? Well, what do you do, Mr. Miller?"

"What do I do? I'm... I'm a writer."

"A writer? Like a journalist? Or an author?"

"An author. I write horror books. I usually self-publish them because they're a little... *strange,* but, every once in a while, someone wants to publish my work. It's a good job for someone like me."

Someone like me—Karen didn't fully understand his statement. She figured he meant he was an introvert and writing allowed him to work alone. She ran her fingertips across his abs as she nuzzled his chest.

She said, "I wish I could have a job like that. Nine-to-five jobs are... terrible. If you help me, maybe I can write something, too. I hear everyone likes erotica..."

Ethan wasn't concerned with Karen's request—it was intrusive but innocent. She really wasn't trying to use him to propel her own career. Ethan just didn't love her, so he couldn't find a reason to help her. He was hoping he'd be able to think rationally by the end of the night—to love her as he did the day prior—but he didn't care about her anymore. The magic was gone.

"A succubus," Ethan whispered.

"What?" Karen asked, baffled. "What did you say? Suc... Suck-u..."

Ethan stared at Karen with a steady glare as she struggled to identify the word. He held his right hand to his face and sobbed—snorting, sniffling, and moaning. *I've missed my chance for true love again,* he thought, *she's one of them, she's a succubus.* He couldn't control himself.

Smiling, Karen sat up in bed and asked, "What's wrong, hun?" She kissed his cheek and caressed his hair. In a soft tone, like a mother teasing her baby, she asked, "Are you okay? Did I hurt you when we were fucking? Hmm?"

Ethan grunted and shook his head. He vigorously rubbed his eyes, then he wiped the tears from his rosy cheeks. He glanced over at his girlfriend and nervously smiled—the corner of his mouth involuntarily twitching. He leaned closer to the edge of the mattress.

As he gazed into Karen's gentle eyes, Ethan said, "Let me... Let me tell you something, sweetie. There are two types of men who cry after sex. Okay, maybe there are a few more, but these two are the most common."

Karen furrowed her brow and asked, "What are they?"

"There's the... the sensitive-type. A person with a lot of, um, *emotion* in him. Too much for his own good, some would say. Then... there are those who are about to kill."

Karen clenched her jaw and cocked her head back. She was caught off guard by the second type. Yet, Ethan continued to smile and snivel. So, she laughed in order to keep a semblance of control—*everything is okay, it's just a joke.*

As he reached under the mattress with his right hand, Ethan said, "*I'm both.*"

He pulled a hatchet out from under the mattress. Karen trembled upon spotting the deadly tool. Before she could utter a word, Ethan flipped her onto her stomach. He grabbed the nape of her neck and pinned her to the bed face-first. He straddled the small of her back, using his body to stop her from squirming away.

Karen screamed, "Stop! Oh, God! Stop! What... What are you doing?! Please, Ethan!"

Ethan released the nape of her neck, then he grabbed the back of her head. He pushed down on her head, shoving her face into the fluffy pillow. Her cries were muffled by the pillow.

Without releasing her head, Ethan held the hatchet over his head, then he struck down at her neck. The sound of a dull, wet thud emerged with the strike. The *mushy* sound continued as he pulled the hatchet out of her neck. Blood gushed from the laceration on her throat, spilling onto the white pillow and bed sheets.

Ethan felt as if he were riding a mechanical bull as

the woman squirmed and flailed her limbs every which way. She violently convulsed, shocked by the brutal attack. She couldn't throw the man off his balance, though.

In a hoarse tone, as if she were choking, Karen stuttered, "Pl–Please, don't... I don't... I don't want to die. Help..."

The author held the hatchet over his head, then he struck down at her neck again. He didn't waste any time, either. He pulled the hatchet out, then he struck her again—*and again.* Blood splattered on his arms, chest, and face as he repeatedly chopped at her neck. The tissue and bone were difficult to cut through, but he was determined.

Karen stopped responding to the attack after the fifth strike, her face buried in a bloody pillow. She only trembled due to the power behind the strikes. The rest of her movements were involuntary. One, two, three... *ten*—it took ten powerful chops to get to the center of her neck. It only took him fifteen more chops to fully decapitate her.

Exhausted, Ethan tossed the hatchet on the floor. He leaned to his left, then he pushed Karen's body off of the bed. The floorboards rattled as her limp body fell to the ground. The killer fell to his side of the bed with his girlfriend's decapitated head cradled in his arms. He wiped the strands of hair away from her face, then he stared at her. He wasn't bothered by her hollow eyes, sunken cheeks, or gaping mouth.

He leaned closer to her head, then he kissed her— a passionate kiss. He licked her lips, he shoved his tongue into her mouth, then he bit her bottom lip. No, her violent death did not bother him. As a matter of fact, it aroused him. He stared down at his crotch and smiled. He was erect—and he looked *slightly* larger than ten centimeters.

So, he placed Karen's decapitated head over his crotch. He jammed his penis into her moist mouth—moist with saliva *and* blood—then he began to thrust. She didn't suck on him, but he could feel the tip of his penis barely scraping her uvula. That sensation made him feel big—it made him feel like a man. He held his breath and his limbs tightened as he ejaculated into the decapitated head.

Ethan sighed in relief, then he lifted her head back to the top of the bed. He wiped the blood, saliva, and semen from her lips.

Teary-eyed, he said, "Thank you for that. I'm... I'm sorry it didn't work out between us. I can't... I just can't be in a relationship with a creature like you—a *monster* like you. Succubi and men, we don't mix well together." He chuckled as tears streamed down his cheeks. He said, "Maybe in another life, maybe if I'm reincarnated as an incubus. Yeah, maybe... Let's just go to sleep now."

He held her head to his chest and placed his chin on her hair. He smiled and closed his eyes. His lips quivered, he wanted to cry, but he focused on sleeping. He counted sheep until he finally dozed off.

Chapter Two

It Didn't Work Out

"Saying goodbye is always the hardest," Ethan whispered as he walked up the stairs, dejected. He wiped the blood off of his hands and forearms using a white towel. He muttered, "Cleaning the mess is harder than making it, too."

The young man stopped at the top of the stairs. He found himself standing in the doorway leading into the kitchen. He glanced over his shoulder and gazed down the stairs leading into the basement. It was melancholic down there—depressing and dark.

He stepped into the kitchen and closed the door behind him. He turned towards the mirror hanging on the wall beside the door. He checked his hands—clean as a whistle—then he adjusted his clothing.

He wore a black button-up shirt with the sleeves rolled up. He carefully buttoned and adjusted his shirt. He also wore jeans and boots—nothing out of the ordinary. He had a few curls in his messy hair, but it never bothered him before. His stubble was fine, too. Women seemed to like it. He wasn't worried about his appearance.

Still, his reflection was pitiful—a broken man roaming a broken world.

With a disappointed expression, a frown and a set of glum eyes, Ethan said, "Look at yourself, Ethan. They like you out there, but they don't *love* you. The succubi... They want to destroy you. They want to drag you along, acting like they love you, but they don't care. You have to be more careful about who you choose to love 'cause they *won't* love you back. You hear me?"

As he continued to fasten his buttons, Ethan's reflection stopped moving. His reflection grinned from ear-to-ear as he leaned closer—while Ethan remained glum. The young author was well-aware of his reflection's ability to move without him. He thought of his reflection as a doppelganger—and it seemed normal to him.

The doppelganger sighed, then he said, "You failed again, pal. You had yourself something special, but you let her slip through your grasp. It's pathetic, isn't it? It's like you *want* to be alone for the rest of your life."

Ethan erratically blinked and stared down at himself, trying to stop himself from crying. He was alone in his home, trapped with his cynical thoughts, but he still did not want to be seen crying. He didn't want to appear weak—even to himself.

He cracked a fake smile and said, "I don't care. I... I wanted it this way anyway. I wanted to... to... to live a bachelor lifestyle for a little longer, you know? I mean, at least I got laid last night, right?"

"*Got laid?*" his reflection repeated. The doppelganger chuckled and shook his head, then he said, "You're not in college anymore, Ethan. It's not about getting 'laid' or slaying as much pussy as possible. It's about finding love. You're a grown man who has never experienced *real* love. You realize that, don't you?"

"I'm only 24."

"So? Mom and dad were in love since they were in high school. They're still together today, too. You're late. You understand me? Where is your love, pal? Where is your princess?"

Ethan stopped fiddling with his buttons, flustered. He dropped his arms to his side and glared at his reflection. His first thought: *let him have it and smash the mirror.* He knew his doppelganger would simply find another reflective surface to contact him, though. He didn't want to cut his hand or elbow, either.

Ethan said, "My love, my true love, is out there. Okay? She's waiting for me to find her. So... I just have to find her."

"I'm not trying to hurt you. That would be stupid. I mean, I'd just be hurting myself if I did that, right? You have to understand something, though: you're running out of time. Soon, all of the good girls will be gone and you'll be left with nothing but succubi. You'll only have 'used-up' women if you don't find *the one* soon."

Ethan absently stared down at his boots, stunned by the blunt truth. He tried to keep his composure, but he couldn't keep his facade afloat. He wasn't lying during the previous night: he was sensitive and he was murderous. He held his hand to his face and grimaced. Tears gushed from his eyes and mucus poured from his nostrils as he sniveled.

He slammed his fist on the wall. The mirror bounced and swayed with the strike. He grunted as he struck the wall again, infuriated.

Saliva spurting from his mouth, Ethan hit the wall and barked, "I will find her! No matter where she's hiding or who she's with, I *will* find her! Do you hear me? I don't care if it takes me forever. Even if I'm fifty and she's fifteen, if she's meant to be mine, *she will be mine.* I will find my true love. I... I can't die alone! I can't–"

A jingly, bubbly tone interrupted his rant. With downcast eyes, Ethan glanced into the kitchen to his left. His telephone, which sat on the counter, was silent and dark. He turned his attention to his right and stared into the living room. The noise was coming from the laptop on his desk—*a ringtone.* He chuckled as he wiped the tears and mucus from his face.

As he approached the desk, he smiled and said, "I... I have a call. I have to take this..."

***

Ethan frowned as he stared at the screen. He wasn't receiving a call from a secret admirer. His doppelganger wasn't messing with his head. The caller ID read: *Mom.*

An image of his mother, Brooke Miller, was shown above prompts to answer or reject the video call. In the image, the middle-aged woman had curly black hair, dark brown eyes, and a few wrinkles on her face. From afar, she resembled any other woman—*nothing special.* Her eyes, dark and sharp, appeared malevolent, though.

Ethan sat and adjusted his shirt, preparing himself for an unpleasant discussion. He muttered, "What do you want this time, mom?" He inhaled deeply, then he accepted the call. He smiled and enthusiastically said, "Mom! Hey, how are you doing?"

Brooke, who appeared to be calling from her patio, smirked and said, "My little Ethan, it's so good to see you. We're doing fine over here. I don't want you to worry about us." She took a sip of her wine—yes, *wine* in the morning. She smacked her lips, then she said, "I know you get annoyed, but I had to call about your date last night. I was awake all night thinking about it, you know? It's exciting stuff, isn't it?"

Ethan blushed as he stared down at his lap and twiddled his thumbs. He didn't know what to say. *I decapitated my girlfriend because I thought she was a demon*—it was nonsense.

Brooke asked, "So, how did it go? Hmm?" She giggled, then she asked, "When's the wedding, sweetie? Am I going to be a grandma any time soon? Huh?"

Ethan sighed, then he said, "We broke up."

"*What?* Are you... Are you kidding me? Please tell me you're joking, Ethan."

"It's not a joke. It wasn't working out between us, so we broke it off. I just... I wasn't feeling any magic with her, mom. I thought it was there at first, but it disappeared last night. It wasn't there anymore. I don't know how to explain it."

"*Magic?*" Brooke repeated in disbelief. She shook her head and rolled her eyes, annoyed. She asked, "What is that even supposed to mean? Huh? I didn't raise a little fairy. You hear me? I raised a *man* and a *man* is supposed to have a family. He doesn't rely on 'magic' to make it happen, he just *does it*. That's how life works."

Ethan stared down at himself, ashamed. When it came to his mother, he was not the confrontational type. He could only sulk and wait until she was done.

Brooke leaned back in her seat and shook her head. She was blatantly disappointed in her son's failure. She wanted to mold him into a family-man so she could continue to spread her genes. Her family line could *not* end at Ethan. She had other opportunities, like Ethan's younger brother, but, if he ended up the same way, she would die off without a large family.

Eyes brimming with tears, she clenched her fist and looked away. Disappointment opened the door to rage. She swallowed the rest of her wine with one loud gulp.

Brooke glared at her son and sternly said, "I am tired of this, Ethan. This is the... the *fifth* time you've failed to tie the knot—to seal the deal. You're running around with these girls, some who are already older than you, but you always mess it up. You just don't know how to please a woman, do you? Your father knows how to pleasure women. Do you want him to teach you? Hmm? What? Do you want him to... to *cuckold* you? Is that what you want?"

With his head slumped down, Ethan ran his fingers through his hair and sniffled. He tried to shrug off his mother's insults, but he was genuinely hurt by her vile tirade. He survived the rampant bullying in school. The insults were worse when they came from family, though. *What kind of mother could bully her own child?*

Ethan grunted to clear his throat. In a cracking voice, he whispered, "I–I messed up. I'm... I'm sorry. I was–"

Disregarding his apology, Brooke said, "I think I need to ask you a *very* serious question before I can continue calling you my son. So, think wisely... Are you gay, Ethan?" Ethan's bottom lip quivered and his eyes welled with tears. Brooke said, "*Answer me.* Open your mouth and talk. I swear, if you don't answer me, I'm going to assume the worst. I'm–"

"*No*," Ethan interrupted. He stared at his mother with an unwavering glare—*please, believe me.* He said, "I like women. I've always liked women, mom. You know that. I just messed up. You wouldn't have liked her anyway. She was a whore. She wasn't pure."

Brooke puckered her lips and nodded as she examined her son's demeanor—he wasn't lying. She was an old-fashioned woman who did not agree with homosexual relationships. Her beliefs weren't exactly developed through religion or hatred, though. She didn't actually care if other men or women wanted to partake in homosexual relationships.

Brooke wanted biological grandchildren so she could spread her genes and beliefs. Homosexuality would lead her to another dead-end and she didn't want that. She was wicked and selfish—and it never bothered her.

Brooke said, "Good. You should only be concerned with getting married and having kids. If you want to be 'gay' or whatever, you can do that *after* the baby is born. Okay?"

Ethan said, "I have to go, mom. I'm very busy. Love you."

Before his mother could respond, he disconnected from the call. Stiff, he stood from his seat and marched into the kitchen. He loudly exhaled, then he panted as he trembled. He was unnerved and frustrated by the conversation.

Veins bulging on his sweaty brow, Ethan muttered, "Why does she care about my sexuality? Huh? It's my life, isn't it? I'm doing it the way I want to do it. She... She told me about the succubi anyway. She did this to me." He approached the cupboard and grabbed a mug. He shouted, "Damn it, she did this to me!"

With the furious roar, he hurled the cup at the wall. The mug shattered into a dozen pieces. He ran his fingers through his hair and paced in the kitchen, visibly upset. He couldn't control his anger. Unfortunately, that meant he couldn't enjoy a nice breakfast at home—*a microwaveable breakfast sandwich.*

He grabbed his keys from a rack and said, "I can't do this. I can't stay here. A diner... Yeah, I'll go to a diner."

Chapter Three

Love at First Sight

Loneliness was a difficult subject. Some people enjoyed lonely days while others loathed the involuntary solitude. It was funny how things worked: the same thing could cause happiness and pain to two separate people. The pain caused by loneliness was only amplified by the happiness of other people—perhaps it was self-pity.

That's exactly what Ethan felt at the diner.

The young man sat by his lonesome at a booth at the far-end of the eatery. Puffy-eyed, he watched the other guests with a blank expression. Families sat in the other booths, enjoying eggs, bacon, and pancakes. A few couples sat at the other tables, flirting while they ate. A drunk homeless man sat at the bar, eating a cheap meal by himself.

That could be me, Ethan thought as he stared at the homeless man, *I could end up just like him.* The life of a lonely hermit was terrifying to him.

"Sorry for the wait. It's been a little busy this morning," a tender female voice said.

Ethan shook his head as he snapped out of his contemplation. He glanced towards his left, then he leaned back. His waitress finally reached his booth—and she was beautiful.

The woman stood five-one with a petite figure. She had silky black hair down to her shoulders and bangs down to her eyebrows. Her dark brown eyes were gentle. She wore a black polo shirt, black pants, and matching work shoes. A black apron with three pockets was tied around her waist, too. Her outfit wasn't glitzy, but she was still very attractive.

Hopeful, Ethan stared at the name tag on her chest. To his dismay, the name was illegible. The waitress pressed on the button on her pen and held her notepad up.

She smiled and said, "My name is Emmy. I'll be your waitress today. Are you ready to order, sir?"

Ethan grinned and chuckled. He opened his mouth to speak, but he could not utter a word. He was rendered speechless by her beauty. He could feel butterflies flittering in his stomach as his heart rapidly pounded in his chest.

The magic was back.

The waitress nervously laughed, amused by Ethan's peculiar behavior. She said, "It's okay if you're not ready to order. I can come back later or someone else will come help you. I'll–"

"No," Ethan interrupted, afraid of missing his chance at love. He stuttered, "I–I'll have... three scrambled eggs, two bacon strips, and the–the hash browns."

"Okay. We'll have that ready for you in ten, fifteen minutes. You want coffee with that? Orange juice? Milk?"

"Coffee. I'll have coffee."

"Okay. I'll be right back."

Before she could leave, Ethan lunged over the table and grabbed her wrist. He pulled her back to the booth, which caused her to stagger. The young waitress yelped as she struggled to keep her balance. Stunned by the patron's audacity, she turned towards Ethan with wide eyes.

She stuttered, "Wha–What are you doing? Please, let me go." Confused by his own actions, Ethan absently stared at the waitress. The young woman said, *"Let me go."*

Realizing he was causing a scene, Ethan released her wrist and leaned back in his seat. He clasped his hands in front of his mouth.

He said, "I'm sorry. I'm *so* sorry. I was just... I was going to ask you for your name. That's all. I just... I just wanted to know your name."

"I told you my name already: *Emmy.*"

"No, I meant your full name. I can kinda see it on your tag, but I can't read all of it."

The waitress stared down at her chest with a furrowed brow. She was surprised to see her handwriting was smudged and illegible. To her disappointment, it was *supposed* to be legible at all times. She feared the patron would report her to her manager if she didn't cooperate. She wanted to avoid that headache.

She said, "My name is Emiko Takahashi. Everyone calls me 'Emmy.' Okay? What's so important about my name?"

Ethan said, "I just... I noticed you were, um... *Asian* or whatever is the politically correct term. Like, uh, Chinese or Japanese or Korean or–"

"I'm Japanese. Asian, Japanese... it doesn't really matter, sir."

Ethan smiled and nodded, blatantly interested. He said, *"Japanese.* I've always been interested in Japanese culture. It's... It's fascinating." He stared down at the table and blushed. He said, "I'm sorry about my aggressive approach. I really didn't mean to grab you like that. My... My name is Ethan, by the way.

Ethan Miller."

Emiko stared at Ethan with a deadpan expression. She was still unnerved by his eccentric behavior. She couldn't read his intentions. He appeared harmless, but there was something about him that was strange. She couldn't put her finger on it. She assumed he was trying to hook up with her. Being fit and attractive didn't give him the right to touch her, though.

She said, "Whatever. It's... It's okay. I forgive you. Your food will be ready in a few minutes."

As the waitress walked away, Ethan joked, "Great. Maybe you can join me when you come back. Huh?" Emiko clenched her jaw and glanced back as she approached the bar. Ethan said, "I'm kidding, I'm kidding..."

Normally, Ethan was a smooth and charismatic young man. He knew how to communicate with women. The waitress made him feel different, though. He couldn't control himself around her. He stuttered and stumbled, unable to keep a cool composure around the waitress. It was an odd feeling, but he welcomed it with open arms.

He watched Emiko until she disappeared around the corner, hidden by the kitchen walls. Giddy, he stared down at himself and chuckled inwardly. He glanced around the diner and grinned. The grim atmosphere vanished. He was no longer jealous of the other couples. In fact, in his mind, every couple was replaced with an image of himself and Emiko.

Love was in the air.

Sitting by his lonesome, he imagined his *entire* life with Emiko. He pictured their early dates—walks in the park, bad movies, and candle-lit dinners. He imagined their wedding, which would inevitably lead to a small family. And, his own family would lead to acceptance from his mother. With Emiko, the future was brighter than the sun.

"Here you go, sir," a male with a husky voice said.

Ethan glanced over at his left and raised his brow. A man in a white, short-sleeve button-up shirt and black trousers stood beside the booth. The bald spot at the center of his head was obvious as he leaned down and placed a mug on the table. The man sniffled as he placed a plate next to the mug.

The man ran his fingers across his mustache and said, "Holler if you need anything."

"*Wait*," Ethan said. The man glanced at the patron with a raised brow. Ethan asked, "Who... Who are you?"

"My name is Burt Baker, sir. I'm the manager here. I'll be personally serving you until the end of your meal."

"Wha–What happened to Emiko? Is she okay?"

Burt sighed in exasperation, then he said, "She's fine. She's busy working in the kitchen. I'd appreciate it if you didn't bother her. Now, please enjoy your meal. Holler if you need anything."

As Burt marched back to the bar, Ethan leaned forward and peered into the kitchen through the pass-through window. He could see Emiko leaning on a counter, chatting with a co-worker.

Ethan leaned back in his seat, lonely and confused. He stuffed his mouth with eggs and bacon as he constantly glanced over at the kitchen with each bite. The perceived rejection struck him *hard.* He was brought down a notch and hurled back into his bleak reality.

Mouth full of food, he mumbled, "Maybe I was

wrong. Maybe she doesn't love me. She's not like the succubi, but she doesn't like me, either. But... But *I* like her. I *love* her. I know I do. Why? Why won't you come see me, Emiko?"

From the back of his head, a soft feminine voice said, "I'm sorry, darling. I can't."

Ethan glanced over his shoulder, startled. He sat in the last booth, so he found himself staring at a wall. He recognized the voice though—*Emiko Takahashi.* Eyes glimmering with hope, he gazed into the kitchen and smiled.

Ethan whispered, "It's you, isn't it? You're trying to talk to me, aren't you? It's... It's telepathy. I thought I was the only one, but... it's really you. You like me. You really like me."

He shoved more eggs into his mouth and stared at the manager—*Burt, that prying bastard.* The pieces were easy to connect in Ethan's unhinged mind: Emiko wanted to be with him, but her boss was keeping them apart. The theory was based off a voice he heard in his head, but he believed it. He was willing to wait for her, too.

As Ethan finished his meal, Burt approached the booth and placed the bill on the table. He was eager to get rid of the bothersome patron.

Ethan pulled his wallet out. The bill came out to $9.69. He could have left a ten-dollar bill and a five-dollar bill to cover the tab and the tip. He wanted to make a statement, though. He placed a hundred-dollar bill on the table. He stood from his seat and tapped the money.

He glared at Burt and said, "That's for Emiko. That's her tip, *not yours.*"

Burt said, "That's fine, sir. The exit is right over

there. Thank you for coming."

Ethan walked away from the manager before the confrontation could escalate. As he strolled towards the exit, he glanced at the pass-through window and waved with a large grin on his face. His newfound love didn't see him, but he could see her. Head over heels, he practically skipped out of the diner and headed to his car—excited for his future.

Chapter Four

Worth A Thousand Words

Emiko Takahashi—it was a very specific name. Surrounding the name with quotation marks and searching through Google, the name yielded over twelve-thousand results. Authors, singers, and everyday people filled the results. Obviously, due to the nature of the name, most of the people resided in Japan. Google couldn't reveal the waitress' identity.

Ethan sat at his desk in his bedroom, wearing only his gray boxer briefs. He logged into his Facebook account. His other friends, who he did not personally know, were insignificant. He searched: *Emiko Takahashi.* He slowly scrolled through the results, but he didn't find his secret lover. So, he refined his search and sorted his results by city.

To his dismay, Emiko did not show up.

He murmured, "Everyone has a Facebook account these days. Where are you hiding, Emiko?"

He leaned back in his seat and thought about their first encounter. He remembered every detail, too. An idea materialized—a bulb illuminated above his head.

He said, "*Emmy.*"

He typed: *Emmy Takahashi.* Then, he limited his search to his city. Lo and behold, he found her at the top of the search results. His fingers trembled as he reached for the mouse. A twisted grin, devious and malevolent, formed on his face. The side of his mouth twitched with excitement, too. He clicked on her name, then he examined every detail of her profile.

Eyes wide with hope, Ethan stuttered, "Sh–She... She's *not* in a relationship." He leaned back, stared at the ceiling, and yelled, "She doesn't have a boyfriend! She's on the market! She's the one! Holy shit! She's the one!"

Trying to contain his excitement, he turned his attention back to the monitor. He scrolled through her posts.

Verbatim, one post read: *I can't sleep. I have class in the morning, then work, but I can't sleep!! No!* (´;ω; `).

Upon spotting the emoji at the end of the post, Ethan smiled and said, "That's cute, Emiko. It's so damn cute."

He scrolled down, then he stopped at another post.

The post read: *I love all of my friends, I really do. Thank you for your help. I miss home, though. I miss mom and dad... They miss me too and it hurts.*

The post brought a tear to Ethan's eye.

Ethan sniffled and said, "I know how you feel, darling. It's hard, isn't it? It's terrible, right? That feeling... That feeling that you're all alone. I don't live in a different country, my family is nearby, but I still feel homesick, you know? You're lucky, though. At least they like you, Emiko. I don't want you to worry about that anyway. You'll always have me."

The author scrolled through her posts. He laughed and cried as he shared her life. He memorized the most insignificant memories—things she probably forgot. Again, he stopped on a picture. It was a picture of food, *of course.* However, the picture linked to Instagram. One thing led to another—that's how things worked.

He opened her Instagram page in a new window and found a trove of pictures. He opened her photo gallery on Facebook, too. He placed the windows side-by-side and searched through her pictures. The images mostly depicted her schoolwork, her dogs in Japan, and food. There were a few pictures of herself, though—simple selfies, outfit-of-the-day collages, and bikini shots.

He loudly swallowed as he leered at her bikini photos. On Instagram, he opened a picture of Emiko in a red, white, and blue bikini. Her chiseled face, slim figure, and perky breasts were perfect to him. On Facebook, he opened a picture of the waitress in a beautiful kimono in Japan. The pictures were different—one traditional, the other carefree—but he was equally aroused by both.

Drenched in sweat, he dropped his boxers and vigorously masturbated. A *squelching* sound echoed over his moans as he tugged as quickly as possible. He wasn't a professional bodybuilder, but the man had more stamina than a crack addict. When he wasn't having sex, he spent hours of his day masturbating. His forearms wouldn't be sore for at least an hour. That didn't mean he wouldn't prematurely ejaculate, though.

Before he could climax, Ethan stopped and held his hands up—as if the police had caught him red-handed. He didn't want to finish. He closed his eyes and performed complex mathematics in his mind to calm his nerves. He was still aroused, but he wouldn't finish early. He took a deep breath and shook his head.

He said, "No, no, no. This is... This is wrong. I can

do better for you, princess. You deserve more than... than *this.* Just give me a minute, okay?"

He scrolled through Emiko's pictures, searching for the perfect image. He stopped upon spotting a picture of the waitress at a beach in Japan. The image only depicted her chest and her head. Her breasts were squeezed together, making them appear larger than usual. However, he was more aroused by her smile—a naughty smirk.

Tears of joy clinging to his eyelids, he whispered, "You're so beautiful. I... I don't know what else to say, but... this is the one. It's amazing."

He wiped the tears from his eyes as he downloaded the picture from her Facebook account, then he printed it out at the highest quality possible. He moved his keyboard and mouse aside, then he placed the printed picture at the center of his desk. His legs wobbled as he stood from his seat. His excitement was difficult to contain.

Towering over the picture, he continued to masturbate. From above, his penis appeared puny—a bad angle. It didn't bother him, though. He was solely focused on Emiko's beauty. He stared at her lips, then he gazed into her eyes. He wasn't looking at an actual person, but he felt a connection to her—*magic.* The magic only made him tug faster.

His dick throbbing in his hand, his body convulsed as he ejaculated on the picture—*a cum tribute,* the first sign of love. His semen splattered on her face and chest, thick and slimy.

Out of breath, he murmured, "Oh, God. That was... That was too good."

He fell into his seat and sighed. He wasn't a virgin, obviously, but masturbating to Emiko felt better than any sex he ever had before. It certainly felt better than sex with Karen. Love—*true love*—made everything feel better.

Nude and proud, Ethan returned his attention to Emiko's Facebook page. From her profile information, he could see she attended a community college near the diner. He occasionally prowled the campus to capture candid videos of students' asses on his cellphone. He just tapped record, then he held his phone under his belt with the lens aiming at the ass he wanted to capture—no one ever suspected a thing.

He stared at a selfie of Emiko at a bus stop. The image caught his attention.

As he analyzed every detail of the picture, Ethan said, "I know that place. I know that bus stop. I can meet you there if you want." He nodded as he stared at the picture, as if he were listening to someone. He said, "No, no. I don't mind waiting all day, Emiko. I'll give you a ride after school. Anything you want, okay? *Anything.*"

He downloaded another picture of Emiko. She smiled as she sat on a bench at her school. Her smile was heartwarming, gentle and reassuring. He taped the printout above his bookshelf, then he hopped into his bed. He had the perfect view of the love of his life. He cuddled with his pillow and stared at the photo, imagining himself with Emiko.

With a beautiful woman watching over him, Ethan fell asleep in comfort.

Chapter Five

Everyone Parties After School

"Where are you, Emiko?" Ethan whispered as he stared at the foyer of the community college. "I've been here since eight in the morning. Did you even have class today? You're not talking to other guys, are you? No, no, no. You wouldn't do that. No, you're a good girl..."

Ethan glanced at the clock on his radio—*12:23 PM*—then he glanced around the area. From his parking space, he could see the administration building, the student store, and a few buildings filled with classrooms. He could also see the same bus stop from Emiko's picture across the street. He had the perfect vantage point of the area.

Emiko was nowhere in sight, though.

Ethan grabbed his tablet computer and leaned back in his seat. He flicked his finger across the screen and browsed Emiko's Facebook page. He searched for more hints about her schedule. Judging from her posts and pictures, he could see she went to school before dusk—she didn't take any night classes. The waitress appeared to work in the mornings on weekends and during the afternoons if she worked on weekdays.

Ethan said, "You have to be around here somewhere. I said I'd wait for you, so I'm going to wait. I just... I wish you'd give me a specific time. I have to work, too, you know? I'm not mad. No, I'm not mad. I'm just a little disappointed. I'll wait, though."

Time passed at a snail's pace. He watched as students entered and exited the school. Students ran down the street and tried to wave down the buses. A few students walked past his car, but no one seemed to notice him—security was conveniently lax. He leered at some of the young women's asses, especially those who wore leggings as pants, but they didn't really arouse him. Sure, he was interested enough to take a look, but he didn't become aroused by watching them.

Ethan glanced at the clock—*2:07 PM.* He leaned closer to the steering wheel and stared at a group of women near a building on top of a hill. With the eyes of a hawk, he could see Emiko was part of the group. The other girls were nothing but a blur to him— *insignificant.* Emiko's glowing beauty blinded him.

He said, "Monday. Two o'clock. I didn't see you get here, but I'll see it next time. I know when you leave, princess." He held his hands over his mouth and laughed deliriously. He whispered, "I'll have your entire schedule soon. I promise, I'll memorize the whole thing, sweetie."

His chest on the steering wheel, he pulled his phone out of his pocket and aimed the camera at the group of students. He zoomed in as close as the app would allow him without distorting the image. She wore a sleeveless gray dress, so he snapped pictures of her bare legs, arms, and chest. Someone made her laugh, so he captured an image of her gentle smile, too. He even tried to take a picture of her feet, but she was too far away to capture a clear image.

All smiles and giggles, Emiko was unaware of her stalker's presence. She accepted Ethan's hefty tip, but she tried to shrug off his outburst at the diner. She acted as if it didn't happen.

Ethan leaned back and sank into his seat, hiding in the shadows of his car as Emiko walked down the hill. She waved at her friends, then she briskly walked across the street to the bus stop—just as he predicted. Sitting by her lonesome, she shoved some earbuds into her ears and played her music. It was the perfect setting.

Ethan smiled and said, "Holy shit. She's alone. She's actually alone. Now's my chance."

He checked his reflection on the rear-view mirror. He adjusted his button-up shirt and picked at his teeth, then he rubbed the stubble on his jaw. He couldn't do anything about his wild hair, so he only hoped she liked his style.

As he gazed at himself, he whispered, "It's now or never, buddy. You can do this."

He pulled out of the parking space, then he slowly navigated the parking lot. He constantly glanced over his shoulder and checked on the bus stop—she was still alone. He drove to the other end of the parking lot, then he took a left onto the street. He cruised at a leisurely pace as his heart raced in his chest.

With each passing second, Emiko grew larger— and his anxiety grew stronger. With his blinkers on, he stopped beside the bus stop. Head down, Emiko was focused on her phone—swiping and tapping. Ethan rolled the passenger seat window down, then he leaned over the center console.

Ethan said, "Hey, Emiko."

Emiko disregarded the car and focused on her phone. If it wasn't the bus, it didn't matter to her.

Ethan coughed to clear his throat, then he shouted, "Hey! Emiko! It's me, Ethan! *Ethan Miller!*"

Emiko pulled the earbud out of her right ear and glanced up at the car. She furrowed her brow and leaned back on the bench, baffled by Ethan's sudden appearance at her school. She glanced to her left, then to her right. She was looking for her friends in hopes of discovering an elaborate prank. They weren't around, though.

She stared into the car and stuttered, "Wha–What are you doing here?"

"I was just driving by and I saw you waiting here by yourself. So, you know, I thought I'd stop by–"

"Are you following me?"

Rosy-cheeked, Ethan huffed and shook his head. He stammered, constantly restarting his sentences. He was being accused of stalking a woman. He was only trying to love her, though.

As he recomposed himself, Ethan said, "I'm... I'm *not* following you. Like I said, I was just driving around the city and I saw you here. It was just a coincidence. I don't know, maybe... maybe it's a sign, too."

"A sign? A sign of what?"

"You know..."

Ethan's eyelids flickered and the side of his mouth twitched. He looked out the windshield as tears welled in his eyes. He could feel a lump in his throat, too—a lump of shame and embarrassment. Breathing deeply through his nose, he fought off the urge to cry.

Ethan said, "Listen, I... I know it sounds strange, but I just stopped because I saw you here alone. I wanted to ask if you needed a ride home or to work... or *anywhere*. It's really no trouble for me. I'm not in a hurry or anything."

Emiko shook her head and said, "No. I'm fine. I don't need a ride. I'd really appreciate it if you left me alone. Thank you."

"Are you sure?" Ethan asked. He chuckled and ran his fingers through his hair, anxious. He said, "It's really nothing to me. I can take you anywhere you want. There's plenty of room in here, too. It's better than taking some crowded bus full of bums and pervs. Come on. Get inside."

"*No.* Please, stop bothering me before I have to—"

A blaring horn echoed through the street. Ethan glanced at his rear-view mirror and frowned. The bus had arrived.

As he rolled forward, reluctant, Ethan asked, "Are you sure? I can drive you. We can... We can look for a party or something. Come on, everyone parties after school. R–Right? *Right?*"

Emiko shoved the earbud into her ear and ignored her stalker. She waved at the bus driver, making sure he wouldn't leave her behind. Ethan was out of options. He took a right and parked at the corner of the neighboring street.

Disappointed, Ethan whispered, "I blew it. Why wouldn't she get in? I've... I've picked up girls before. What... What's wrong with her?"

Misty-eyed, he stared at his rear-view mirror. He could still hear the bus' coughing engine. He rubbed his eyes as the bus departed from the stop. He refused to quit his pursuit—it was out of the question. He glanced over his shoulder, then he did a U-turn. He returned to the street and followed the bus.

As he stared at the back of the bus, he whispered, "*Bus 6.* She takes Bus 6."

Following two cars behind, Ethan trailed the bus and checked each bus stop. He wouldn't quit until he found Emiko's next destination.

Chapter Six

The Afternoon Shift

Ethan leaned forward in his seat, weaving and bobbing his head like a short person at a concert. The bus was parked at a stop near the diner. He could connect the pieces: a bus, a waitress, and a diner meant Emiko was taking public transportation to her job. He needed absolute certainty, though.

Ethan bit his bottom lip as the light turned green. The bus was still parked at the stop and he could not see who was getting off. He hopped in his seat as the driver behind him honked. He reluctantly cruised forward, his eyes locked on the bus stop.

As he peered through the bus windows, Ethan whispered, "Emiko, there you are..."

His theory was correct: Emiko walked to the diner to begin her afternoon shift. The young author took another U-turn, then he entered the parking lot across the street. The parking lot was used by the neighboring department store and small shops, but it was empty—business was slow. He parked at the edge of the lot with the perfect view of the diner across the street.

He sighed in relief, then he said, "I'm lucky, Emiko. *We're* lucky. I didn't lose you." He held his hand over his face and broke down into tears. He mumbled, "I thought... I thought I lost you. I thought you were trying to get away from me. You just can't be seen with me yet, right? You want me to watch you, *right?*"

He pulled a handkerchief out of his pocket and

wiped his nose. He tried to compose himself. A grown-man crying in the parking lot of a 99-cents store was never a good sign. He tightly closed his eyes with each blink as he tried to focus his vision. He leaned on the steering wheel and stared at the diner. Thanks to the large windows, he could see most of the eatery. He couldn't see the kitchen, but he could see the dining area.

Emiko pranced from table-to-table, genial and helpful. She had changed from her dress and tossed on her generic uniform. Unlike her experience with Ethan, she didn't seem bothered by any of her customers. She kept a genuine smile on her face— and Ethan loved it. Her uniform, conservative and generic, was outshined by her smile.

The author grabbed his phone and aimed the camera at the diner. He had to hold his phone over his head to take pictures over the passing cars. He had a steady hand, though. All of those years of excessive masturbation and voyeuristic photography conditioned his arms. He snapped pictures of Emiko from afar. The quality wasn't the best, but he could make-do. He flicked his finger across the screen and examined the photos.

He whispered, "Emiko, Emiko... You're so damn beautiful. I mean, I... I don't know what to say. I'm a writer, right? I should know how to tell you how beautiful you are, but I can't. You're too beautiful for English words. Maybe something in Japanese can accurately explain your beauty. I'll find out soon."

He glanced up at the diner. He watched as Emiko chattered with a family. He knew she was a nice person, he could see it in her eyes, but he couldn't tell if she was playing a role for higher tips. It didn't bother him, he just didn't want her to suffer. He could only imagine the hardships she went through working at a diner. *Miserable,* he thought, *she must be absolutely miserable.*

Ethan said, "When we're together, you won't have to work like... like *this.* You won't have to serve people like some sort of slave. I'll take you away from the working class. You understand me, sweetie? You won't have to work for tips like some... some stripper. No, you won't have to work at all. You can just take care of our family while I bring us up to the upper-class. Does that sound good to you, Emiko? Yes, it's perfect, isn't it?"

The sensitive man sighed and rubbed his eyes. He placed his chin on the steering wheel and stared at Emiko from afar. Her beauty caused him to whimper. *How could someone be so perfect?*–he thought. He stared down at his pants and chuckled. He had an erection. The love of his life wasn't even trying to titillate him, but he was still aroused.

"Do it," a soft female voice said at the back of his mind.

Ethan stared at Emiko and responded, "Now?"

"*Now.*"

"Okay, okay. I've never done this before, but I'll do it. I'll do it for you, okay?"

Ethan's fingers trembled as he unbuckled his pants, tears dripping from his eyes with each blink. His dick, stiff like a flagpole, popped out of his fly. He leaned on his door with his left arm over the window while he stroked himself with his right hand. He spent most of his time watching Emiko. However, he couldn't help but glance around every once in a while.

A man crying at a 99-cents store parking lot was

one thing. A man masturbating in a 99-cents store parking lot... Well, that was a whole 'nother story.

As if the woman could hear him, Ethan whispered, "Emiko, it feels so good." He moaned and shuddered, overwhelmed by the feeling of ecstasy. His breath breaking with each pant, he said, "I'm going to... to cum."

He held the handkerchief over his penis and ejaculated. He caught the gooey streams in his hanky. He took a minute to catch his breath, then he shoved his penis back into his pants and the handkerchief back into his pocket.

Ethan said, "Thank you, Emiko. Thank you for everything."

Satisfied, he leaned back in his seat and stared at the diner. He was prepared to wait until Emiko's shift ended to continue following her.

***

The sun fell beyond the horizon. The sky was orange and blue, like every Hollywood movie poster. Cars of all shapes and sizes cruised down the street, heading in every direction. A few angry drivers honked and argued with each other, yelling about politics and society, while others recorded the confrontations. Emergency sirens on fire trucks and police cruisers occasionally blared through the area, but no one seemed to notice the stalker in the parking lot.

Ethan sat in the driver's seat of his car. He took a sip of his coffee, which he purchased from a neighboring donut shop. He kept his eyes on his love the entire time, too—she still served customers with a smile. He glanced at the clock: *6:09 PM.*

He leaned forward and whispered, "Here we go..."

Emiko jogged down a walkway, then she skidded to a stop beside the crowded bus stop. She leaned forward and stared over the cars parked on the side of the street. She sighed in relief—her bus was barely arriving. She could be seen talking to an older woman as she shuffled through her bag, laughing and smiling. She was perpetually friendly.

A good girl like that couldn't possibly hate anyone—including Ethan.

"Come on over," the feminine voice whispered at the back of Ethan's mind. "Don't be scared, darling. I don't bite."

Doe-eyed, Ethan stared at Emiko and nodded. He pulled on the parking brake and said, "I'm coming, sweetie. I'm–"

He paused as the bus pulled into the stop, blocking his view of Emiko. He blinked erratically and shook his head. He was disappointed in his failure to act. He wasn't given much time, but he still felt as if he had missed his chance.

As the people boarded the bus, Ethan reversed out of his parking and murmured, "I missed you too many times already. I have to see you..."

He drove to the farthest exit behind the bus, then he pulled into the street. He drummed his fingers on the steering wheel as he followed the bus. Just like the bus, he stopped at each bus stop and watched as the passengers exited the vehicle. He was led away from the busy commercial district, taken deeper into a residential area.

Apartment buildings, some five stories tall, surrounded him. The apartments weren't luxurious, but they were adequate for most common needs.

As the bus pulled into another stop, Ethan stopped

his car behind a column of parked vehicles—hidden in plain sight. He leaned over the passenger seat and stared at the bus with narrowed eyes, carefully watching every movement in the large vehicle. An elderly woman, a man in a janitor's uniform, a few teenagers and... *Emiko*—Emiko hopped off the bus.

Ethan smiled and whispered, "Hey, sweetie... I thought I lost you."

Eager, he climbed out of his car, then he jogged onto the sidewalk. He trailed behind the young woman. He glanced around the area. The street sign read: *Madison Street.* The buildings in the area resembled each other. He could memorize each crack on the bricks, though. He only needed to know where Emiko lived and it would stay on his mind until the end of time.

Unaware of her stalker, Emiko strolled into a five-story apartment complex to her right. Ethan jogged to catch up, glancing every which way. He walked through the front door and found himself in a hallway. Emiko was nowhere in sight, though. *She couldn't have gone inside so fast,* he thought, *it's impossible.* He glanced over at his right.

He whispered, "Stairs..."

He ran up the stairs and slid into the hallway on the second floor. He quickly slid back behind the wall upon spotting Emiko. He peeked around the corner. The young woman stood in front of the third door to the right, wrestling with her bag and keys—still oblivious.

As the door closed, Ethan shambled down the hall and approached the apartment. He stared at the number above the door: *26. 26*—two digits, easy to remember. He smiled and leaned closer to the door.

He could hear her moving about inside of the apartment. He smiled from ear-to-ear—the type of smile a father would have as he met his newborn baby for the first time.

With a grin on his face and tears in his eyes, he whispered, "What are you doing in there, baby? Huh? Do you need a hand? Do you want me to come in? Just say the word and I'll come in. Come on, talk to me again. Say–"

"Can I help you, sir?" a man asked from over Ethan's shoulder.

Ethan casually glanced around the hall, acting as if he were lost—*playing stupid.* He glanced back at his uninvited guest.

A short, portly man stood behind him. The man wore a filthy gray polo shirt, black trousers, and scuffed dress shoes. He had a bald spot at the center of his head, too. He sniffled and coughed, blatantly sick. The careless man didn't even cover his mouth.

The man chuckled and snorted, then he asked, "Can you hear me? *Hello?*"

Ethan stuttered, "Wh–Who are you?"

"Who am I? My name is Charles. I'm the manager of this apartment complex. Now, who are *you?* I don't think I've ever seen you around here before."

"You're the manager?" Ethan asked. He laughed and shook his head, relieved. He said, "I'm sorry. I might be in the wrong building. I was looking for a friend's apartment."

"I'm sorry, too, pal. I can't help you with that. I don't just hand out the tenants' information to 'friends' like that. You're going to have to get out of here and give your friend a call. Go on, kid. I can't have you hanging around here like some sort of stalker."

"I get it. I'll go. Thank you for your time."

As Ethan took a step towards the stairs, the manager sneezed. Mucus dripped over his lips and saliva splattered on the wall.

Ethan smiled and said, "Here, take this." He pulled the handkerchief out of his pocket and handed it to the manager. He said, "I used it a little, but... Well, you're already sick anyway. Might as well clean yourself up."

Charles nodded and said, "Yeah, yeah. Thanks, pal."

Ethan smiled as the man rubbed the cum-soaked handkerchief on his lips and nose. The manager even used the handkerchief to blow his nose. Fortunately, thanks to his clogged nostrils, he really couldn't smell the semen on the hanky. His lack of taste didn't allow him to taste the cum, either. It was a win-win situation.

Satisfied, Ethan waved at Charles and said, "I'll just have to contact my friend later. Have a nice day, sir."

"You too."

Ethan walked out of the building. He was amused by his devious actions, but he was dismayed by his failure. He was stopped before he could cross the finish line. He wanted to enter Emiko's apartment, but he couldn't cause a scene. He hopped into his car, then he peeled out of his parking spot.

Chapter Seven

Insomnia

"I'm beginning to think this is all just some... some fucked up game," Ethan said as he paced back-and-forth in his kitchen.

He grabbed a fistful of his hair and tugged on his head, delirious. He was tormented by his cynical thoughts and irked by his uncontrollable shifts in mood. One moment, he was happy and hopeful about his future; the next, he felt as if the entire world was going against him.

He was an unhinged young man who was shunned by his family and friends. He didn't get the help he needed, so he continued to descend into his own secluded world of depravity. He stopped in front of the mirror.

As he stared at his reflection, Ethan said, "*Twice.* That's two times that she's rejected me. I... I keep hearing her voice in my head, she's telling me that she loves me, but she keeps pushing me away in person. It's insane, isn't it? What the hell is going on here?"

His reflection responded, "It's you, Ethan. It's not her. You're just not confident enough for a girl like that. You're *asking* instead of *demanding.* 'Do you want a ride? Are you sure?' That's no way to talk to a girl like that. She wants you to be more assertive. She doesn't want some passive chump."

"I–I don't understand. This... This is me. Acting like *me,* like *myself,* has always worked for me. Wha– What's happening? What's changed?"

"The world is changing. People want different things. You can't stay the same forever and expect to please everyone. The gentleman-type is out. Women are attracted to bad guys... again."

Ethan stared at his reflection, teary-eyed. He licked his lips, then he clenched his jaw. He carefully examined himself, reading the expression on his face as if he were looking at another man. Of course, in his mind, he *was* looking at a different person—his doppelganger. He didn't know if he could believe himself or not.

As a tear streamed down his cheek, Ethan said, "I've had sex plenty of times. We both know that. Even if times change, even if Emiko is a different breed, I can adapt. I can still have her."

His reflection responded, "You better start working on it, Ethan. I don't think a *fairy* like you can get a girl like that..."

"I can."

"I don't know..."

"*I can!*"

The apartment was dominated by silence. A news channel was playing on the TV in the living room, but the noise was muted. His unadulterated anger caused the racket to stop.

"You... have... to... listen," the feminine voice whispered at the back of his head.

With the message, the volume increased on the television and the racket outside returned. Ethan glanced around the home, searching for the source of the voice. He was alone, though. He heard Emiko's voice in his head before, but it was different in his house. The woman was nowhere in sight.

As he stared at the ceiling, the disturbed author

whispered, "It's you, isn't it? Emiko, you're trying to talk to me, aren't you? Telepathy... It really is telepathy." He opened a window in the living room, then he sat on the windowsill. As he stared at the houses across the street, peering towards Emiko's neighborhood, Ethan said, "Talk to me. I'm listening."

The sound of coughing engines, obnoxious kids, and domestic disputes dwindled. The world came to a grinding halt—silence reigned supreme.

Dancing into his ears, the feminine voice said, "Watch your TV. Watch me."

Ethan furrowed his brow upon hearing the message. As if he were in a trance, he shambled into the living room, then he fell onto the sofa. He increased the volume on his television. A reporter stood in front of a suburban house and spoke about a missing thirty-year-old woman—*Karen.* The news was insignificant, though. It didn't bother him.

He asked, "What am I supposed to be looking for? What–"

He stopped as Emiko walked onto the set. She approached the reporter, then she yanked the microphone out of her hands. With her glowing eyes, dark but beautiful, she stared at the camera and smiled—such a friendly smile.

She said, "Hi, Ethan. I'm sorry I have to talk to you like this. As you know, I'm stuck in my apartment and Charles didn't let you in. I'm sorry about treating you like trash out there, too."

Ethan leaned forward as he stared at the television in utter awe. He responded, "I... I forgive you."

Emiko sighed in relief, then she said, "I'm glad. I thought you hated me..."

"No. No, I could never hate you, princess. I just... I

didn't understand why you were acting the way you acted. That's all."

"I owe you an explanation, don't I? I love you, Ethan. That's the truth. I'm just too embarrassed to admit it. I can't do it in front of everyone."

"Wh–Why? What's wrong?"

Emiko blushed as she stared down at herself, bashful. She kicked the rocks under her boots and twirled her hair. Ethan's bottom lip quivered as he watched her. Her shy demeanor aroused him.

Emiko glanced up at the camera and said, "I'm pure, Ethan. I've never had a boyfriend before. I've never... Jeez, this is so embarrassing, but... I've never had sex before. I'm a virgin." Trembling with excitement, Ethan held his hand to his mouth and chuckled inwardly. Emiko continued, "If I become your girlfriend, I have to hide it from everyone because I can't let my family back home find out. They wouldn't accept it and they'd force me to go back... without you. I don't want that."

"I don't want that, either. I can keep our love a secret, I swear. No one has to know about it. Not even you..."

Ethan pushed the coffee table aside, then he fell to his knees. He crawled forward and approached the television. He planted his lips on the screen, passionately kissing Emiko's lips. Playing along, Emiko puckered her lips and pretended to kiss the camera. He couldn't physically feel her lips, but he felt her love.

As Ethan leaned away from the TV, Emiko said, "I wish that was real..."

"What do you mean?"

"Come to my apartment, Ethan—*tonight*. Kiss me.

Touch me. Make love to me while I sleep. Just... Just don't wake me up. I want to believe I'm still pure when I wake up. I want all of this to be a secret in the morning. Okay? Like you said: no one will ever know, not even me."

Ethan touched the screen, as if he were caressing Emiko's hair. He said, "I can do that, princess. I can give you everything you ever wanted."

"Really? Even a... a family? I've fantasized about having a family with you, you know..."

"Me too!"

Ethan and Emiko shared a laugh, tears of joy coursing down their cheeks. Ethan was elated by Emiko's confession. Emiko appeared pleased to share in Ethan's happiness. Of course, the waitress wasn't *actually* talking to him. The unhinged man believed it, though.

Ethan said, "I'm going to pay you a visit, Emiko. I'm going to make your... No, I'm going to make *our* dreams come true. I'll be there in an hour, maybe two. I just need to get some supplies first. You get some sleep, okay?"

Emiko nodded and enthusiastically said, "*Okay!*"

She walked off the screen and the reporter returned. As if nothing had happened, the reporter continued discussing the details of Karen's mysterious disappearance. Shrugging off the peculiar event, Ethan staggered to his feet. He lurched into his bedroom and began organizing his supplies.

Chapter Eight

To Make Love

Ethan arrived at Madison Street. He parked three buildings away from Emiko's apartment, his sedan hidden under a tree away from the streetlamps. A few vehicles and pedestrians still wandered the streets, hopping between bars or finally heading home from work. Yet, the neighborhood was still relatively tranquil after midnight.

Ethan stared at his reflection on the rear-view mirror and said, "This is it. There's no turning back. Make her proud."

He nodded, determined. He grabbed a black backpack from the passenger seat, then he hopped out of the car. He breathed heavily as he approached the building, trying to keep a semblance of control— *just a student going home, nothing to see here.* He walked through the front door and stared down the hall, the backpack slung over his shoulder.

To his delight, the coast was clear. He briskly walked up the neighboring steps, skipping a stair with each lunge. The second-floor hallway appeared to be empty, too. The manager was seemingly absent, likely knocked out by his nighttime cold medication. Although the corridor was empty, he still had to remain quiet in order to avoid any nosy neighbors.

"26," Ethan whispered as he approached the third door to his right.

He gazed at the door with curious eyes, marveling at the barrier as if he had just discovered an ancient artifact. He planted his ear on the door and listened—*silence.* Silence was good. It meant she was not near the front door and he was free to enter.

He leaned down and examined the locks. An old-fashioned pin tumbler lock appeared to be the apartment's best defense. Unfortunately for Emiko, the lock had been outdated for years—and Ethan knew exactly how to bypass it.

"Easy-peasy, easy-peasy," Ethan murmured as he reached into his bag.

He pulled a lock-pick set out of the smallest pocket. He took one final glance down the hall as he knelt down in front of the door—the coast was still clear.

Lock picking was a simple task. He pulled the tension wrench and the rake out of the set. He inserted the tension wrench into the bottom of the plug, then he placed *slight* pressure on the wrench. He continued by shoving a rake with three ridges into the hole above the wrench. He placed a little more pressure on the wrench as he moved the rake back-and-forth—*like a rake.* With the gentle movements, he was able to slowly rotate the wrench. *Click*—and the door was unlocked.

Simple.

He performed the same process on the second lock. Upon unlocking it, he turned the knob and gently pushed on the door. To his utter relief, Emiko did not set the latch lock on the door. He quietly slinked into the home and closed the door behind him.

Ethan found himself in the living room of the small apartment. A console table hugged the wall to his left. There was a small seating area and a flat-screen television to his right. Over the bar and the archway, he could see the kitchen directly ahead. He leaned to his right and stared at the wall to his left. Towards the center of the wall, a hallway opened up and led to the other rooms in the apartment. The home was quiet and simple.

The author slipped out of his shoes, then he tiptoed forward. He examined a stack of letters on the console table. The letters were addressed to Emiko Takahashi—some were local, others were international, none were open. Although he was invading her home, he 'respected' her privacy and left the letters alone.

He walked past the sofa and approached the entertainment center. Particularly, he examined the stack of movies sitting next to the small flat-screen television. All of the Blu-ray covers depicted couples about to kiss, but never actually kissing—*cliché romance films.* He preferred horror, but he didn't mind exploring other genres.

Ethan whispered, "We can watch these later, babe. I'll make your life just like a movie..."

He glanced down the hallway—*silence.* He entered the kitchen, then he opened the refrigerator. A person's appetite could shine light on a personality. Chicken, meat, cheese, fresh vegetables, and 100-percent fruit juice filled the fridge—no soda, no beer, no junk food. Her diet appeared to be healthy—healthier than most.

The intruder exited the kitchen and tiptoed down the hall. He grimaced with each shrill creak from the floorboards. Still, it sounded as if he were the only person walking in the home. He stopped at the first door to the right, which led to a small bathroom. The sink, the toilet, and the bathtub-shower combo were clean—she took care of her home just as she took care of herself.

There was something dirty in the bathroom, though: *the laundry hamper.*

Ethan swallowed the lump in his throat, then he shambled into the room. He grabbed fistfuls of the dirty laundry with his trembling hands. He held the panties, bras, and t-shirts up to his mouth and nose, then he took a large whiff. The scent of a woman lingered on the clothing—and it aroused him profusely.

He shuddered as he rubbed his crotch. Like a dog at the dinner table, he whiffed and trembled with excitement. He couldn't control himself. His bottom lip quivered as he licked the crotch of a pink thong—*delicious.* He shoved the pink thong into his pocket and tossed the rest of the clothes into the basket. He tried to organize the dirty laundry, hoping Emiko did not have a photographic memory like him.

In a nervous whisper, Ethan stuttered, "It–It's fine... It's fine." He patted his pocket and stuttered, "Th–Thank... Thank you for the... the gift."

He returned to the hallway, struggling to keep his composure. He opened the first door to the left. He found himself staring into a small storage closet. He already had her underwear in his pocket, so he wasn't interested in her coats. He thought about sniffing her high heels, but he fought off the peculiar urge.

Ethan rubbed the nape of his neck as he approached the final door to his right. He stared into the room, amazed. The computer desk, the dresser, the shelves on the walls... None of it mattered to him. He only focused on the queen-sized bed at the center of the room.

Emiko slept peacefully on the bed, covered in a red blanket as she nuzzled a white pillow. The straps on her blue nightgown could be seen over the blanket. Her hair was tied in a tousled bun, too. In her sleep, her natural beauty shone like the sun on a summer day. Her elegance brought tears to Ethan's eyes.

Overjoyed, Ethan whispered, "I'm... I'm here. *I'm home.*"

***

Ethan inhaled deeply, then he tiptoed into the room. He carefully placed his backpack beside the bed, then he knelt down as if he were about to pray before going to sleep. He pulled a particulate mask out of the bag, then he put it on. The mask covered his nose and mouth. He pulled a handkerchief and a bottle of ether out of his bag. He poured the ether onto the handkerchief.

Ethan leaned closer to Emiko's face. He gently rubbed the handkerchief on her nose and mouth. He didn't want to suffocate her, he only wanted to knock her unconscious. He knew it wasn't like the movies. He had to hold the moist cloth over her face for a few minutes before she was really knocked out. The effects of the ether wouldn't last very long, either.

Realizing she was unconscious, the intruder placed the hanky on the neighboring nightstand. He pulled the blanket off Emiko's body, then he leered at her figure. He stared at her chest—he could see her erect nipples through her nightgown. He turned his attention to her bare legs, then to her feet. He glanced at Emiko's face, making sure she was truly unconscious, then he started lifting her nightgown up to her belly button—*an outie.*

He reluctantly pulled his mask down to his neck as he leaned forward. He couldn't resist. He kissed her stomach, then he licked a circle around her bellybutton. He moved down and pecked at her thighs. He stopped down at her feet. The man had a foot fetish—and Emiko's feet were freshly pedicured. He licked her soles, then he sucked on her toes. A *slurping* sound echoed through the room, but Emiko did not awaken.

Ethan moved up and kissed her legs. He stopped at her waist, then he kissed her crotch—planting his lips on her blue underwear. Yet again, he was fully erect and ready to go. He could have pulled her panties down and raped her, but he didn't want to taint her. He was convinced that she was a virgin. She would wait for him as long as he waited for her—or so he thought.

He shook his head and whispered, "No, not yet. Not like this. I have to... I have to give you what you asked for."

Ethan dabbed her face with the handkerchief again, making sure she stayed unconscious during the imminent procedure. He returned the moist handkerchief to the nightstand, then he riffled through his backpack.

He pulled a jar filled with semen out of the bag. The small jar held approximately 25-milliliters of semen—nearly an ounce of cum, or 4 ejaculations on a good day. He carefully placed the jar on the floor. He wouldn't be able to fill it if he spilled it. He reached into his bag, then he pulled out a needleless syringe with a plunger and a tube.

Artificial insemination: the act of injecting semen into a vagina without sexual intercourse.

Ethan knew all about artificial insemination. Again, it wasn't like the movies. He couldn't just *jam* a turkey baster into her vagina and fill her with his semen. No, the process required *finesse.*

He drew back on the plunger with nothing but air, then he pushed down on the plunger—the syringe was ready. He slowly sucked the semen into the syringe. He gently tapped the syringe in order to get rid of the air bubbles. He didn't want to fill her vagina with air after all, he wanted to fill her up with his semen.

Ethan dabbed her face with the handkerchief again—she was still unconscious. He grabbed her shoulder, then he rolled her onto her stomach. He grabbed one of the pillows and placed it under her waist in order to raise her hips, then he took off her underwear.

He stopped for a moment as he ogled her genitalia. He spread her cheeks as he stared at her clean pussy and anus. He smacked his lips like a starved man waiting for his meal, eager for a taste of her cinnamon ring.

He shook his head and whispered, "Stop it, Ethan. It can wait. You have to wait, okay?"

Misty-eyed, he rapidly blinked as he tried to clear his vision. He connected the needleless syringe to the tube, then he shoved the other end of the catheter into Emiko's vagina. He guided the tube to her cervix, then he pushed down on the syringe's plunger. He attempted to fill her uterus with his semen.

As he stared at his semen, Ethan whispered, "Go get 'em, little guys. Make us proud."

Upon finishing, he pulled the tube out of her vagina. He tossed the supplies into his backpack, then he pulled a white wand massager out of his bag—*a vibrator.* Artificial insemination worked best with an orgasm.

Fortunately for Ethan, a state of awareness was not required for orgasms.

The wand buzzed as he pushed on the switch. He held the wand between the pillow and Emiko's clitoris. He occasionally moved it up-and-down, he even thought about shoving his fingers into her vagina, but he didn't want to wake her with his movements. He was taking a very dangerous risk already. Sweat dripped from his brow as he gently shook the vibrator under her clitoris. He was simultaneously excited and terrified.

On one hand, he enjoyed pleasuring his lovers; on the other, he was afraid of getting caught. Still, he figured if a privileged college student could get out of trouble after raping a drunk student, he could evade the law as well. He snapped out of his contemplation as Emiko trembled. Her thighs and ass jiggled a little as her toes curled. She didn't moan loudly, but she was undeniably having an orgasm.

Ethan whispered, "*Beautiful.*"

He turned the wand off, then he shoved the vibrator into his backpack. He returned all of the remaining supplies—the jar of cum, the bottle of ether, and the hanky—to his bag. He lifted Emiko's underwear to her waist and pulled her nightgown down, then he flipped her onto her back. He tossed the pillow up to the headrest, too.

Everything was returned to its proper place.

Ethan lifted the blanket up to her chest and whispered, "Thank you for inviting me to your home, princess. When you wake up tomorrow, you will still be pure. I'll keep our love a secret, too, okay? I'll check up on you over the next few weeks. I'll make sure the baby is doing well. Our family is going to be perfect, I promise." He smiled and kissed her, planting a tender kiss on her lips. As he tiptoed out of the room with the bag slung over his shoulder, Ethan said, "Good night, princess. I love you."

Ethan tiptoed his way out of the apartment and crept out of the building. Like a shadow at night, he wasn't seen or heard by anyone. He hopped into his car and absconded from the crime scene, hurtling towards a brighter future.

Chapter Nine

Happy Birthday!

"You look beautiful today, sweetie," Ethan said as he stared at Emiko from afar.

Ethan sat in the driver's seat of his car in the parking lot beside the diner. The sky was overcast with clouds, rain poured onto the city and cascaded down the windshield, but he could still see the love of his life in the eatery.

Emiko, unaware of her stalker's presence, smiled as she helped her patrons. She was molested by Ethan only two weeks earlier, but she didn't realize it. Despite the frigid weather and the special circumstances of the day, she still wore her plain uniform with pride—what a woman.

Why was the day special? Well, it was November 26, 2016. According to her Facebook profile page, it was Emiko's birthday.

Ethan said, "You look beautiful every day, but... you're shining today. Twenty-one years old... You turn *21* today, princess. That's special. It's very special. It's when we become real adults. I... I brought you something to celebrate. I hope you like it."

He nervously smiled as he patted his chest. He hid Emiko's gift in his coat's interior pocket—just thinking about it made him feel giddy. He took a deep breath, then he climbed out of the car. He pulled his coat over his head and jogged to the entrance of the diner. The bell chime echoed through the eatery as the door swung open.

Ethan glanced around the diner, searching for his love. A few patrons lingered in the booths, the tables, and the bar. It wasn't as busy as before, though. Emiko had conveniently retreated into the kitchen before he arrived, too.

Another waitress, a brunette woman, beckoned to Ethan and said, "You can seat yourself, sir. I'll be right with you."

Ethan nodded and followed her directions. He didn't want her as his waitress for the day, but he didn't want to cause a scene, either. He sat at the last booth to the left—the same booth where he first met Emiko. It seemed appropriate.

As he twiddled his thumbs and stared at the table, Ethan whispered, "Emiko, Emiko... Come on out. Please, come out. Just tell them we're friends. Tell them we're *really* good friends. Please, come out and talk to me. Come–"

"Sorry for the wait," the brunette waitress said as she approached the booth. The peppy woman smiled and said, "My name is Patricia. You can call me 'Patty' if you'd like. I'll be your server today. I can get you a drink now while you look over the menu. What will it be?"

Ethan responded, "No, um... No offense, but I'd really like it if Emiko served me—*Emiko Takahashi.* Can you send her out here? Please?"

Patty furrowed her brow, baffled by the customer's request. She had never had someone ask for a specific waitress at the diner. She glanced over at the kitchen, then back at Ethan.

She said, "Emmy is on her break right now."

"I can wait."

"O–Okay. Well, I'll... I'll ask her to come see you as

soon as she's free. Let me know if you need anything in the meantime."

"Thank you, miss. Again, no offense. I just prefer Emiko's service."

"Okay..."

As Patty departed from the kitchen, Ethan simpered like a misbehaving child. He pulled his coat open and peeked into his pocket. He hid a black ring box in the pocket. There was a 10-karat white gold diamond promise ring inside of the box. He considered purchasing something more expensive, but he didn't want to appear 'obsessive' around Emiko.

"What are you doing here?" Emiko asked as she stood beside the booth, her arms crossed as she tapped her foot like a disappointed parent.

Ethan said, "Emiko, it's good to see you. I was–"

"I thought we were done with this?" Emiko interrupted in an uncertain tone.

"Done with what?"

"Done with *this.* I don't understand what you're doing here. I don't even want you to be here, either. I... I just don't want to see you, okay? I don't want to be mean, but... I *don't* want to see you. That's all. Please, leave."

Caught off guard by Emiko's hostility, Ethan responded, "I... I understand the problem, Emiko. You have to say that because..." He leaned closer and whispered, "Because they're listening and they don't want us to be together. But I *know* we're meant to be together. I understand, Emiko. I know how to play their game."

Emiko stared at Ethan with a furrowed brow— curious, baffled, *terrified.* She was conflicted by a mishmash of emotions. She was afraid of Ethan's unhinged mind, but she also pitied the young man. She couldn't conjure the words to respond to his bizarre claims.

Ethan smirked and whispered, "Listen, we can just tell everyone we're friends until we're ready to tell them the truth. Okay? Everything will be fine that way. Trust me."

Grimacing, Emiko responded, "I don't know what you're talking about, but you're really starting to scare me. I think you should leave before we have to call the cops."

"The cops? Why?"

"Please, leave before–"

Ethan held his index finger over his lips and waved his other hand—*shush.* He could see Emiko was about to scream for help. He believed she was trying to play the role of a reluctant lover. She was playing it a bit too authentically for his liking, but he forgave her.

In a soft tone, Ethan said, "Okay, okay. I didn't realize it had to be that much of a secret. I get it, though. I'll get out of your hair in a minute and no one will ever suspect a thing. I... Well, I have a surprise for you. Close your eyes."

Emiko did the opposite. She glared at Ethan, refusing to even spare a blink.

A sheepish smile on his face, Ethan shrugged and whispered, "Or don't..." He pulled the gift out of his pocket, then he opened the ring box. Balancing the box on his palm, Ethan presented the ring to Emiko and said, "Happy birthday."

Emiko stared at the expensive ring, then she glanced at Ethan. The ring caught her off guard—she had never received such an expensive gift from anyone outside of her family. However, she was more concerned with Ethan's message: *happy birthday.* The baffled expression on her face spoke volumes about her thoughts: *how the hell does this man know about my birthday?*

Noticing Emiko's reluctance, Ethan said, "I want you to have this. It looks expensive, but it really wasn't that much. So, don't worry about the price or anything like that. It's not an engagement ring, either. It's just a, you know... a promise ring. Go on, take it."

Emiko said, "*No.* I don't want your gifts. I don't want *anything* from you, sir."

"Wha–What? I don't understand. I did what–"

"How did you even know it was my birthday today? Hmm? I never told you that. I don't even know you. Have you... Have you been stalking me?"

"No, no, no. I would *never* do that, Emiko. I just... I... Look, I don't know what to say. I just wanted to give you a gift for your birthday. That's all. I didn't think it would bother you. Hell, I didn't *want* it to bother you. Why would I want to do something like that to someone like you?"

Emiko shook her head, befuddled. She couldn't read Ethan's intentions. She understood his words, but she didn't understand the reasoning behind his actions. He appeared gentle and bashful, but she was not pleased by his persistent pursuit. She couldn't take any risks. She wasn't trying to hurt him, but she didn't want to give him any false hope, either.

There was no relationship between the pair—and she had to make that clear.

Emiko shouted, "Burt! Burt, I need you out here! *Now!*"

Ethan sighed in disappointment, then he muttered, "Burt... Damn it..."

Burt emerged from the kitchen, wiping his hands with a white towel. He casually marched towards the booth, then he stopped upon spotting Ethan. The manager clenched his jaw and inhaled deeply through his nose, clearly frustrated.

Burt asked, "What are you doing here, sir?"

Ethan responded, "I was coming in for a meal and I thought I'd give Emiko a gift for her birthday."

"It's true," Emiko said. "But I don't want his gift and I don't want him here. He's bothering me, just like last time."

"No, I'm not. I just told you that I'm not trying to bother you. I'm trying to do the opposite. How could you say that about me?"

"That's enough," Burt interrupted in a stern tone. He jabbed his index finger at Ethan and said, "I want you to get out of my diner. Today, tomorrow, and the next day. You're not welcome here anymore. You understand me? I'm calling the cops if I see you anywhere near my diner or my employees. Get up and get out."

Ethan stared down at the ring box, disappointed. He returned the gift to his coat pocket, then he stood from his seat. He gazed into Emiko's eyes, begging for a chance to talk without uttering a word—*please, don't do this to me.*

Burt grabbed the nape of his neck and pushed him away from the booth. Ethan lurched towards the center of the diner, barely keeping his balance.

Burt shouted, "Don't look at her like that! Get out of here!"

As he staggered to the exit, Ethan waved at Emiko

and said, "I'm sorry. I didn't want it to be like this. I'm so sorry. I'm going to fix it. I'm going to fix *me.* I promise, I'll be a better man in the future. I'll be... I'll finally be good enough."

Ethan sniveled as he stepped into the rain. He didn't cover his head with his jacket or his arm. He just shambled to his car—soaked and disappointed.

As they watched him from the diner, Burt said, "You need to get rid of that guy, Emmy."

Eyes full of pity, Emiko watched as the sedan peeled out of the parking lot. She said, "I really don't know him."

"Well, then you should really think about calling the police and making some sort of report. You don't know what these creeps are capable of until they actually do something. By then, it's always too late... Go ahead and take a few minutes for yourself. Holler if you need anything."

"Thanks."

Emiko vacantly stared at the rain cascading on the windows. She thought about Ethan's bizarre actions while considering Burt's advice. The police wouldn't be able to protect her at all times, but contacting them would bring a sense of security to her life. She vowed to call the cops after work.

Chapter Ten

Dinner

Emiko hopped off the bus. Hands stuffed in her coat pockets, she slowly walked down the sidewalk. After the confrontation at the diner, she was cautious of everyone and everything. She waited until the bus drove off, then she approached her apartment building. She stopped on the porch, then she glanced around the neighborhood.

Vehicles still trudged up-and-down the streets while pedestrians wandered the sidewalks. The sun was falling beyond the horizon and darkness would arrive within fifteen minutes. There were no suspicious characters in sight, though. She didn't see any men sitting in parked cars or hiding behind trees.

She nodded and whispered, "Everything's fine..."

Emiko sighed in relief, then she entered the building. She waved at the manager, who was heading up to the third floor, then she approached her door. As far as she was concerned, she reached the finish line—she was safe. She entered her apartment, making sure to lock the door behind her. She didn't forget the latch lock.

She planted her moist brow on the wall beside the door and sighed as she took off her shoes. She wiggled her toes and moaned as she massaged her feet. Serving customers for hours was a physically demanding job. She took off her coat, revealing the gray long-sleeve shirt she wore underneath.

As she went to hang her jacket on the neighboring

coat tree, Emiko stopped moving. Wide-eyed, she vacantly stared at the wall in front of her. The coat slipped out of her fingers and fell to the floor. Tears materialized in her eyes, sweat glistened on her brow. She trembled uncontrollably as her breathing intensified.

A *sizzling* sound emerged from the kitchen—but she lived alone.

Emiko glanced over at the kitchen. She swallowed the lump clogging her throat and held her bag close to her chest, then she tiptoed forward. She walked around the sofa and leaned towards her right. She stopped and stared into the kitchen over the bar, shocked. She couldn't scream, she couldn't run. The young waitress was paralyzed by her fear.

Ethan stood near the stove, cooking fish in a pan. He wore a white button-up shirt, black trousers, and matching dress shoes. His hair was straightened and combed to the right. His cologne, a mossy aroma, could be smelled from the living room. He appeared relaxed, too. The confrontation at the diner didn't seem to bother him.

In fact, the disturbed author even set the table before Emiko arrived. The plates and eating utensils were neatly set at each side of the table. A candelabra with three lit candles sat at the center of the table. It was a romantic setting for an important night.

Surprised, Ethan hopped and gasped upon spotting Emiko in the living room. He indistinctly muttered and chuckled, humiliated by his melodramatic reaction. He lowered the heat on the stove, then he approached the bar. At that moment, Emiko wished she had quietly walked out of the apartment before he noticed her. She needed a new escape plan.

Ethan said, "Jeez, Emiko, you scared me. You should really try announcing yourself when you get home. Anyway... I thought you'd be home a little later. The food isn't ready, but I could fix up an appetizer or a–"

"What are you doing in my apartment?" Emiko asked.

She clenched her jaw as she tried to stop herself from sobbing. She tried to keep a semblance of control around the intruder. She couldn't allow him to exploit her fears.

In a stern tone, Emiko asked, "What the *hell* are you doing in my home?"

Ethan held his hands up in a peaceful gesture. He smiled and said, "I'm just making dinner, you silly goose. Things didn't go so well at the diner 'cause of your stupid boss, but that doesn't mean the day has to end on a bad note, right? We can still celebrate your birthday."

"I'm calling the cops."

With a concerned expression, Ethan walked to the archway and responded, "The cops? Why? What's the matter?" Emiko reached into her bag and stepped in reverse. As she searched for her cellphone, Ethan asked, "What's wrong? Did someone follow you home?"

Upon hearing the questions, Emiko stopped riffling through her bag. Eyes welling with tears, she glanced up at Ethan in utter awe. She could see he was sincere. She realized the man was truly deranged.

Ethan approached the windows in the living room. He glided his eyes across every inch of the street, searching for any potential stalkers.

He said, "This isn't a great neighborhood, sweetie. I mean, it's not the worst you can do, but... I don't know, I just don't like you living here by yourself. Perverts are everywhere these days. When the prisons get filled up, the government lets those psychos out first. They think that they'll actually follow directions—that they've been rehabilitated. They're not, though. They cut their bracelets as soon as they're free. You have to be careful around here, Emiko."

Emiko sobbed and stuttered, "You–You're scaring me..."

"What? I'm on your side, remember? I'm–"

As he spoke, Emiko pulled the phone out of her bag. She swiped her finger across the screen as she ran around the coffee table. Her fingers trembled as she tried to dial 911 while lurching towards the front door.

Before she could reach the exit, Ethan tackled her and pinned her to the wall—pressing his body against hers. He plucked the phone out of her clammy palm while covering her mouth with his other hand.

"Stop it," Ethan said, his face an inch away from hers. He said, "Don't scream, don't fight. If you do, the *bad* people will hear you. That man that was following you, he could be standing outside of your front door. He could be listening to everything. Don't worry, though. I'll protect you. You don't need the police, you only need me."

Ethan grimaced and gasped as Emiko bit his hand. Emiko kicked his shin, but she couldn't hurt him because she wasn't wearing shoes. She lurched towards the front door, but to no avail. Ethan tackled her again, grabbing her legs and pulling her to the floor.

Emiko yelled, "Help! He–"

Ethan flipped her onto her back, then he straddled her stomach. He covered her mouth with his hand, then he leaned closer to her face. He could see the unadulterated fear in her eyes, but he didn't understand it. *What is she afraid of?*–he thought.

Teary-eyed, Ethan said, "I'm not trying to hurt you. I've... I've just been doing everything you told me to do. I did it because I... I love you. *I love you,* Emiko." A tear dripped from Ethan's eye as he blinked, plunging onto Emiko's cheek. He said, "I'm going to move my hand now. Okay? Don't scream. Just... Just say: 'I love you, too, sweetie.' Okay?"

Ethan lifted his hand from Emiko's mouth. Emiko wheezed as she gazed into Ethan's eyes. Letting him off easy didn't seem to work, so the blunt truth was her only option.

She said, "I don't love you. I don't even remember your name. Please, just leave me alone. Don't hurt me."

"Wha–What? N–No, you... you love me. You... You said so on the TV. You remember that, don't you? You said you loved me. It's supposed to be a secret, remember? I know you love me, Emiko. Just say it."

"No... I don't love you. You're crazy, mister. You're fucking crazy..."

Stunned by the rejection, Ethan shook his head and stuttered, "B–But, I got your messages. Your messages, they were real..."

"*Messages?* I never sent you a thing..."

"Your messages," Ethan repeated.

Emiko clawed his face, digging her nails deep into

his skin. Ethan leaned back and placed his palm over the bloody cuts on his left cheek. Emiko raised her hips and tried to toss the intruder off her, but to no avail. So, she tried to scratch his face again—she missed him by a fingernail.

As she slapped and scratched at his face, Emiko yelled, "Help! Please, help me! There's someone in my apartment! Help!"

Infuriated, Ethan struck down at Emiko's brow with his elbow. His elbow hit the side of her forehead, which caused the back of her head to slam onto the floorboards. Dazed by the hit, her eyelids flickered and her head swayed. He hit her again with his elbow, trying his damnedest to hit the same place on her brow. The second blow knocked her unconscious.

He leaned back and dug his fingers into his hair as he stared at his loving girlfriend. He was bothered by her rejection and angered by her yelling. He glanced over at the door, then towards the ceiling—*nothing.* He didn't hear a single footstep in the building.

He whispered, "I have to get you out of here, princess. This place is... *toxic.* It's not good for you. That's why you're acting like this. You need to come home." He leaned down and kissed her lips. He said, "Happy birthday, darling."

Ethan grabbed her ankles and dragged her to the front door. He ran back into the kitchen and turned off the stove, then he blew out the candles. He grabbed his coat and bag, too. He couldn't afford to leave any evidence of his presence in the apartment.

With all of his supplies, he returned to the front door and whispered, "We have to work fast and we have to make it look natural, okay? Let's just, um... act like you're drunk or something, okay? I know, I know, you're not that type of girl. We need to do this, though. Come on."

Ethan lifted Emiko from the floor. Fortunately, the woman was small and slim so she was easy to carry. He lifted her from her waist and tossed her arm over his shoulder. He lugged her out of the apartment, her feet sliding across the floor. There was no one around in the building to see them, either. He safely absconded with her unconscious body.

Chapter Eleven

Welcome Home

Emiko awoke, cold and disoriented. The side of her head stung, bruised due to the beating. She lay on a white blanket, heartbeat thrumming in her ears. Her vision was blurred and the room was dark, but she knew she was staring at a ceiling. It wasn't the ceiling of her bedroom, though.

As she sat up, she whispered, "What happened?"

She glanced around the area, searching for something she could recognize—but to no avail. The young woman found herself in a small room—a five-by-eight-foot room. She sat on what appeared to be a designated sleeping area—the blanket on the floor.

To her right, water dripped on the floor from a shower head installed on the ceiling. On the wall to her left, a filthy toilet was anchored to the floor. The rest of the room was empty.

Emiko crawled forward, then she stopped. When she moved, the sound of a chain rattling emerged in the room. Wide-eyed, she glanced down at her feet. Her right ankle was shackled. A heavy chain connected to the shackle led to the wall behind her. She glided her fingertips across the chain, as if she were checking if it were real.

To her utter dismay, the chains were not a figment of her imagination. Her arms trembling uncontrollably, she tugged on the chain with all of her might. She leaned back and tried to use all of her body weight against the chains, but to no avail. The chains clicked and clanked, but she couldn't break free. The wall mount was as durable as the steel chains, too.

Emiko stammered, "N–N–No... Th–This... This can't be happening."

She glanced at the makeshift shower, then at the toilet. She couldn't find any tools to help her escape. As her vision adjusted to the darkness, she noticed a door on the parallel wall from her bed. The door appeared to offer the only possible escape route from the room. She crawled forward, then she gasped as she fell to the floor. The chain was short so she couldn't reach the door. It was out of her grasps.

At the top of her lungs, Emiko screamed, "No! God, no! Somebody help me! Please, help!" She wheezed and sobbed as she planted her nose and lips on the concrete floor. Her voice cracking, she stuttered, "H–Help me. Please... Please, don't hurt me. I don't want to... to be here anymore. I'm sorry if... if I did anything wrong. Just let me go."

She stopped crying and sniffled as she glanced up at the door. The sound of footsteps seeped into the small room—heavy, creaky steps, like those of someone walking down a flight of stairs. The footsteps stopped, then a *click* sound followed. Light poured through the gap under the door, partially illuminating the small room.

Emiko whispered, "Is... Is someone there?"

She crawled in reverse as the door swung open, slipping and sliding until her back hit the wall behind her. She held her hands over her face and closed her eyes. The light temporarily blinded her—and she was scared of meeting her captor.

"Hey, Emiko," a man's voice said, soft and caring. "You can open your eyes, princess. It's okay. I'm not going to hurt you. You're safe now."

Emiko opened her eyes to a squint as she slowly lowered her arms. She grimaced and whimpered, awed by the revelation. She could only hope she was dreaming.

Ethan stood in the doorway, a light shining behind him. He still wore the same clothing from the failed birthday dinner, albeit with a few more wrinkles. Judging from the grin plastered on his face, he didn't seem bothered by the situation. He had a young woman chained up in his basement, but he acted as if everything were normal.

Emiko leaned to her left and stared past Ethan's figure, searching for an exit. She could see a washing machine hugging the wall behind him. Women's clothing dangled out of the washing machine. She recognized a shirt—the shirt she was wearing when she was kidnapped, but she didn't recognize the bra. A few cardboard boxes were stacked beside the machinery, too. The boxes appeared to be stained with a dark liquid—*blood.*

The pieces were difficult to connect for a sheltered woman. She knew she was being held captive—that much was certain. She appeared to be trapped in a makeshift bathroom built in a basement, too. She couldn't figure out Ethan's goals, though. She thought: *is he going to rape me? Is he going to kill me? Has he killed before?*

Emiko stared down at herself, disappointed and frightened. She furrowed her brow and tilted her head upon noticing her outfit. She was wearing her blue nightgown. The fact sent her into a tailspin of confusion. She was knocked unconscious, stripped down to her birthday suit, and dressed again—*what else could have happened?*

Upon spotting the doubt on her face, Ethan entered the room and crouched in front of Emiko. He said, "I went back to your apartment and got you something cozy to wear. I didn't... I didn't do anything else to you, I promise. I just wanted to make you feel comfortable."

"Will you let me go?"

"Wha–What?"

Emiko gazed at her captor with tearful eyes. She repeated, "Will you let me go?"

"No... No, I can't do that. Not now, at least. You know, it's not part of the plan..."

"What are your plans? What are you going to do to me?"

Ethan sighed as he stared down at the floor. He ran his fingers across the frigid concrete as he thought about his response. He didn't want to appear too 'clingy' around Emiko, but he wanted to show his love. Honesty, balance, and cooperation were integral to all relationships—he knew that very well.

Ethan explained, "This is *your* room, Emiko. I made it a long time ago, but, believe me, you're the first to ever sleep here. It's a special place—a place for people I trust. I want you to stay here until... until you can openly admit that you love me. No more secret messages, no more public rejections. Okay? I just want to believe that you love me."

"B–But, I don't love you. How... How could I love you if I don't even know you? I'm sorry, but... that's impossible. It's... It's crazy. No, I don't love you."

"You see, that's what I'm talking about, Emiko. I know you love me, but you're just bottling it inside for some reason. I need you to let it go. You need to understand that love is natural, no matter what your family thinks. I don't want you to be embarrassed anymore."

"*Embarrassed?*"

Ethan sighed in disappointment. He was hoping for the easy way: Emiko would realize her love for him, he'd unchain her, then they'd start their life together—*a fairy tale.* Unfortunately, Emiko opted for the hard way. It was going to be a challenge, but he was willing to accept it—for true love.

As he stared at the floor, Ethan said, "I've spent a lot of time thinking about our future together, princess. The past few weeks... They've been a roller coaster for me, but I've enjoyed the ride. I think we'll both enjoy where this roller coaster takes us. We're going to have a big house with one of those *huge* backyards. We'll start off slow and 'practice' by getting a dog. We can get, um, one of those Shiba Inus from Japan. You know, it'll help with your homesickness, right? Then, we take the big step: we'll have mixed kids. These kids, they'll lead the world away from the darkness. Yeah, they'll get rid of racism and all of that bullshit... It's a beautiful vision of the future, isn't it?"

Ethan paused for a moment, lost in thoughts of the future. Emiko shuddered and panted, terrified by her captor's erratic behavior.

Ethan swallowed loudly, then he said, "In order to create that future, I have to break down the barriers blocking our love. You understand me? I have to find a way to... to... to let our love flourish. That means we have to get past your fear and hesitation. You have to love me so I can love you."

Emiko asked, "Are you ever going to let me go?"

Ethan chuckled, then he responded, "You won't have to go anywhere if you don't want to, sweetie. We'll have maids and nannies to take care of everything. That's part of the future, too. Maids and nannies... They'll take care of everything for you."

"You... You won't let me go now? Not even to look around the house?"

Ethan sighed and shook his head—*nope.*

Emiko said, "My family... I have a family. My father, my mother, my brother... They'll be looking for me. They're going to *miss* me. My brother is twelve years old. If you hurt me, he–he won't understand why I never came home. It'll break their hearts. You... You can't do this. It's crazy."

"I'm *not* going to hurt you."

Emiko couldn't say another word. She held her hands over her mouth, grunting and groaning as she sobbed. She fell forward and landed in Ethan's arms. She cried into her captor's chest, mumbling about her family and her fears. She was hopeless and helpless.

Yet, Ethan couldn't help but smile as he felt her warmth. She was crying, but her tears didn't bother him. Despite the circumstances, her embrace was enough to warm his cold and lonely heart. He stroked her hair and shushed her—*everything's going to be okay.*

Seizing the opportunity, Emiko lunged forward and chomped at Ethan's shoulder. Ethan lost his footing and fell back, so Emiko was only able to bite his shirt. Before she could maul him, Ethan quickly crawled in reverse until he slipped through the doorway. The captor emerged from the attack unscathed.

He staggered to his feet and said, "This is what I'm

talking about. You can't be doing that. You don't *have* to do that. I obviously have to help you realize that, don't I? You'll learn. Yeah, you'll learn over time." He glanced at the stairs to his left. He said, "I have to go now. I'll be back tomorrow, okay? I have to finish writing my book."

Emiko crawled back to the bed in the corner. She stared at Ethan with a blank expression—cold and steady. She refused to speak to him under the horrific circumstances. She wasn't going to become a lover or a friend, she wasn't going to fall to Stockholm Syndrome.

As if he believed he impressed her, Ethan smirked and asked, "What? Didn't I tell you? I'm a writer. Like, a *published* author. Maybe I'll come read something for you someday. I think that would be nice. I'll see you soon. I love you, Emiko."

Ethan closed the door, sealing his captive with the darkness. He locked the door with his keys—no one was getting in or out without him. He walked up the stairs, prepared to continue the rest of his day— normal, like yesterday.

Upon hearing the creaky stairs, Emiko lunged forward and shouted, "You bastard! You sick bastard! Let me go! You can't do this to me!" She wheezed and groaned, horrified. She cried, "Please... Please, *let me go!*"

Of course, her screams—insults and pleas—were ignored. She yelled and cried as she tugged on the chain, but to no avail. She could not escape the shackles. She was trapped in the dungeon, left by her lonesome.

Chapter Twelve

The Perfect Life

The sound of jingling keys and the tumbler lock emerged in the room—a terrifying alarm. Wide-eyed, Emiko sat up on her blanket. She stared at the doorknob as she scooted closer to the corner. She hoped to see a police officer in the basement—a knight in shining armor. At heart, she knew the man of her nightmares was returning.

The door swung open.

Ethan shoved the keys into his pocket as he stood in the doorway. The young man smiled, genuinely happy. He walked into the room, then he squatted down in front of Emiko. He gently chuckled as she scooted closer to the corner. She exhibited fear, but he misinterpreted it as shyness. He liked her bashful personality.

The author reached forward and stroked her hair, shoving the strands away from her brow. He moved down and caressed her cheek.

He said, "It's okay. I'm not going to hurt you. You see? I'm one of the good guys. Everything–"

Emiko chomped at his fingers. Agile, Ethan pulled his hand away and fell back. He narrowly dodged her attack. Although Emiko did not chase him, he crawled to the other side of the room. He sat in the corner diagonal from Emiko.

Ethan said, "You don't want to do that, Emiko. If you bite me, I'm going to put a muzzle on your face. You act like a dog, you get treated like a dog. Okay? I swear, I'll find a way to lock a muzzle onto your head so you *never* try to bite me again. Besides, even if you bit my chest or my finger, even if you *ripped* one of my fingers off, you would accomplish nothing. It wouldn't kill me, it wouldn't set you free. It would only make me angry. Don't risk it. I don't want to hurt you."

I don't want to hurt you—those words sent shivers down her spine. She crawled back to the corner, retreating from the confrontation and accepting a temporary defeat. Her captor was correct anyway—hurting him would not save her. She would have to kill him if she really wanted to escape, but she wasn't a killer.

Ethan said, "I was afraid to come down here. I brought you home last night around nine. You woke up around midnight. At least, that's when I first heard you scream. It's... It's now two in the afternoon. You missed breakfast because I ignored you. I wanted to apologize for that."

"What were you doing?" Emiko asked, infuriated. "Huh? Were you stalking more people?"

"No, I don't 'stalk' people. I'd never do something like that," Ethan responded. As Emiko huffed and rolled her eyes, the captor said, "I was trying to write a chapter for my new book, but I couldn't do it. The words weren't coming to me. I've got a severe case of writer's block—and that makes me angry. When I get angry, I hurt people. I hurt them very badly. I don't want to hurt people because I am... *inadequate.* Believe me, I'm not a bad person. I just do bad things sometimes..."

Emiko gazed at Ethan, baffled. His intentions were difficult to read, like a book written in a foreign language. He appeared harmless, but he obviously caused harm to her. Yet again, she found herself simultaneously despising and pitying her captor. However, she figured she could manipulate him during his most vulnerable state.

As he stared at his hands, brooding, Ethan said, "I think we started off on a bad foot last night, so I want to spend a nice, romantic day with you. I'm sure that will help me clear my mind. It'll even help you clear yours. Okay?"

Emiko took a deep breath and nodded. The opportunity landed on her lap, like a present from a loved one—wrapped with a bow on top.

Playing along, Emiko stuttered, "Th–That sounds good. Can we... Can we spend the day outside? I could use some fresh air."

"Outside?"

"Yes, outside. We don't have to go far. We can go to your backyard and... and have a little picnic. You like picnics, don't you? I love them. Can we have a picnic outside? *Please?*"

Ethan smiled and said, "I like picnics, too."

Emiko nervously giggled upon hearing the response. Her hope was rekindled—for a moment. Unfortunately, the smile was quickly wiped from her face.

Ethan said, "We can have a picnic in here—in your room. It'll be a romantic *indoor* day."

Trying to fight the urge to cry, Emiko grimaced and said, "A picnic has to be outside. Besides, it can't be romantic in a dungeon like this, right?"

"What?" Ethan asked as he glanced around the room. He rubbed the nape of his neck and said, "I guess it's pretty dark in here. I thought it looked okay, but I can fix it up if you want. Maybe I'll install a light, add some decorations, make it pretty."

"I want to leave. I want to go outside. Please, take me outside. We need to trust each other, right? That's how love works: *trust.*"

"You're right, but you just haven't earned that privilege yet," Ethan said as he staggered to his feet. He approached the door and said, "We'll start the day with a bath, then we'll have dinner."

"A–A bath?"

"Yeah. I'll be right back," Ethan responded as he strolled out of the room.

Emiko stared at the door, awed. *A bath for him,* she thought, *or for me?*

***

Ethan returned to the room, gripping the bail of a stainless-steel bucket in his right hand. The bucket was filled with boiling water—steam emanated from the liquid. A loofah, a bottle of shampoo, and a bottle of body wash floated in the water, too. He placed the bucket on the floor and knelt down in front of Emiko.

He said, "Take your clothes off and crawl into the shower."

"N–No..."

"Don't make this difficult, sweetie. If you cooperate, I'll let you bathe yourself. If you don't... Well, I'll have to bathe you. I don't want to put my hands on you until you're comfortable, but I won't have you stinking up the place. Okay? Get undressed and slide into the shower. *Now.*"

Teary-eyed, Emiko closed her eyes and shook her head. She refused to take a shower in front of Ethan, standing her ground in spite of the dangers.

Ethan said, "I don't want to hurt you, but I will if I

have to."

Emiko panted upon hearing Ethan's warning. She couldn't keep her facade afloat, she couldn't masquerade herself as a resilient woman. She held her hands to her face as she grimaced and sobbed. Her sorrow echoed through the home, but it did not change her captor's course of action. Trying to comfort herself, the same phrase echoed through Emiko's head: *he's seen it before, he's seen it before, he's seen it before.* She slowly lowered the strap of her nightgown. The garment fell, revealing her breasts.

Ethan's eyes widened as he leered at her bare chest. He licked his lips as he stared at her light pink nipples. He imagined himself sucking on her teat like a newborn baby. He dropped his hands over his crotch, hopelessly trying to hide his erection.

Emiko couldn't keep her composure. She stopped disrobing and crossed her arms, covering her chest. She knew he already saw her naked, but it was different while she was conscious.

Tears trickling from her eyes, Emiko stuttered, "I–I can't do it..."

"Just take it off, Emiko. It's normal."

"This *isn't* normal. Please, just let me go."

Frustrated, Ethan lunged forward and pulled on her nightgown. Emiko cried and flailed her limbs, trying to fight off her attacker while covering her breasts and crotch. The other strap ripped, then the garment slipped across her figure. A loud shredding sound emerged as the rest of the nightgown ripped down the middle.

Ethan rolled the garment into a ball, then he tossed it outside of the room. He turned the knob next to the door, which caused water to pour out of the shower head on the ceiling. He checked the water with his hand—lukewarm.

Ethan said, "It's perfect for you."

He wiped his wet hands on his jeans, then he extended his arm towards Emiko—*go ahead, take my hand.* Emiko sat in the corner, her arms wrapped around her legs and her face buried in her knees. The couple stared at each other—confused, frustrated, furious.

Ethan grabbed Emiko's arm, then he dragged her into the makeshift shower. Emiko fell to her side under the water. She didn't fight Ethan. Instead, she peacefully accepted the shower. The water brought a sense of normality to her world. She felt filthy, worn and gross. She was afraid she was sexually abused while she was unconscious, too. The water washed away the uncertainty in her mind.

Ethan poured some body wash on the wet loofah, then he scrubbed Emiko's body—all while Emiko vacantly stared at the wall. He vigorously scrubbed every inch of her figure, from her head to her soles.

He stopped and said, "You're dirtier than I thought. You're going to need hotter water. Don't move."

Emiko squirmed and whimpered as Ethan turned the knob near the door. Scorching water spewed from the shower head. The searing droplets of water caused her skin to redden. Yet, the woman did not attempt to leave the shower. She had given up on the idea of escaping.

As he scrubbed her, Ethan gritted his teeth and said, "I have to... *cleanse* you, princess. I have to clean all of the shit you might have rolled in when we weren't together. I know it hurts, it burns like hell, but you have to go through this if you want to prove yourself to me."

He stopped scrubbing and sat back on his heels. He breathed deeply through his gritted teeth, hissing like a snake as he waved his wet arms. Red and sensitive, his hands and forearms were also burned by the hot water. He persevered, though.

As he observed her fidgety body, Ethan said, "I want to believe you're a virgin, Emiko, but it's hard. These days, everything is about sex. The 'news,' the TV shows, the movies, the music, the books... It's all about sex. I mean, books about sadomasochism sell more than extreme horror stories—and that's just not right." As he massaged shampoo into her hair, Ethan said, "In today's world, I don't know if a woman can stay a virgin after her thirteenth birthday. In fact, I don't know a *single* woman who was able to keep her legs closed after thirteen. You whores... You filthy whores, all of you!"

Emiko stared at Ethan with bloodshot eyes. She was awed by the man's misogynistic speech—a vile rant fueled by hatred. His shifts in mood were eerie, too. She couldn't tell if he loved or hated her. Still, she stayed quiet.

Emiko panted as Ethan rolled her onto her back. Scorching water coursing every which way on her figure, her nipples were erect and her milky white skin was riddled with rosy patches. She gasped as Ethan separated her legs.

Ethan glared at her bare crotch, blinded by his rage. Like a person with an obsessive-compulsive disorder, he had an inexplicable urge to clean *everything.*

Without taking his eyes off her crotch, he dragged the bucket closer to the shower. The water in the bucket was boiled before he entered the room. The temperature of the water was well above 200-degrees before the shower. The temperature had dropped to 160-degrees by the time he reached for the pail. The scalding water was enough to cause third-degree burns—and Emiko wasn't aware of that.

Ethan lifted the bucket from the floor. He stared at his captive's bottom half, as if he were contemplating his next move, then he dumped the water on Emiko's crotch. Emiko shrieked at the top of her lungs as the searing water streamed across her crotch and vagina. The bloodcurdling screech echoed through the home.

Ethan struck Emiko with a closed fist—a fast, powerful jab to the face. Emiko continued to flail her limbs and scream. So, Ethan struck her again. He cried as he hit her four more times with all of his might, water raining onto his head and shirt. He stopped his assault as blood leaked from Emiko's busted nose. She twitched and groaned, defeated.

As he staggered to his feet, Ethan sniffled and said, "That... That's enough of that. You–You're clean now." He approached the knob and turned off the water. Teary-eyed, he said, "I'm... I'm sorry about hitting you. It was for your own good. Don't worry, I'll make it up to you, okay? I'll go get your clothes, then I'll finish dinner. I'm... I'm sorry."

Emiko did not respond. She lay on the floor and vacantly stared at the ceiling—dazed by the attack. Lips painted with blood, hoarse breaths escaped her mouth as she shuddered uncontrollably. She could not feel her crotch. As a matter of fact, she felt nothing at all—no pain, no emotion, *nothing.*

Disappointed in himself, Ethan walked out of the room with his head down. He locked the door, then he proceeded with his plans.

***

"I knew it would look good on you," Ethan said as he ran his eyes over Emiko's figure. "I guess everything looks good on you. You're just gorgeous, princess. You're the most beautiful woman on the planet. I'm a lucky guy."

Emiko sat in the corner of the room, her wet hair swept over her shoulder. She wore a sleeveless black dress with a v-neckline. The tight dress perfectly gripped her petite figure. Her outfit was simple but elegant. However, clothing could not cover the dried blood under her nostrils or her swollen lips—a garment could not heal her wounds.

Ethan placed a tray on the floor between the couple. He shoved the tray closer to Emiko's bed. Two plates and two cups sat on the plastic tray. Grilled chicken, steamed vegetables, and white rice were piled on the plates. The cups were filled with water. In order to prevent an escape or an attack, the eating utensils on the tray were plastic. The meal was supposed to be healthy in order to make Emiko feel like she was home.

It didn't work.

Ethan shoved a spoonful of rice into his mouth. He loudly chewed his food, smacking his lips like a parched camel. He smiled and beckoned to Emiko as he reached for his chicken—*go ahead and eat, it's safe.* To his dismay, his date did not devour the fresh meal or guzzle the cold water. Her lack of appetite was worrisome.

Ethan asked, "Did I do something wrong?"

Emiko furrowed her brow as she stared up at Ethan. *Did I do something wrong?*–she was stunned by the audacious question. She was kidnapped, restrained, and brutalized by Ethan, but he still had the nerve to ask such a disrespectful question. She couldn't utter a word. She was violated—*defiled*—by the unhinged man.

Ethan pushed the tray closer to Emiko. He said, "I made this meal just for you, sweetie. I know what you like. Please, *eat.*"

Emiko slowly shook her head as she scooted closer to the corner. She was hungry, but she refused to eat the meal.

Ethan loudly swallowed, then he said, "Please. It's good for the baby."

"*The baby?*" Emiko repeated, baffled.

The author gazed at Emiko's stomach. For a moment, he considered telling her about the artificial insemination. If he succeeded, her pregnancy would be reaching the fourteenth week. He needed her to eat to ensure the child would be healthy at birth. He couldn't tell her the truth, though. An honest confession would paint him as a monster—and he couldn't do that.

Ethan took a bite of the chicken and said, "I'm getting ahead of myself. I'm sorry about that. I mean... If we're ever going to have a baby—far, far in the future—you need to be healthy. Having a baby is the hardest thing on the planet. It's a miracle that only females can provide thanks to their strength and, of course, their sexual organs. It's... It's amazing. Please, eat the food. Stay strong and healthy."

Who are you?–Emiko thought as she gazed into Ethan's moist eyes. One moment, the man was spewing a vile rant about women; the next, he was praising women for their resilience and strength. He was impossible to read. Despite his kindness, Emiko remained hesitant. Doubt clouded her mind, fear burdened her shoulders. She stared down at her body—she couldn't tell if something were different about herself.

How could she trust the man who kidnapped her?

Ethan grabbed a spoonful of rice from Emiko's plate, then he held the eating utensil closer to her mouth. On his knees, he slowly scooted closer to the young woman. He didn't want to alarm her with any sudden movements.

Emiko whimpered as the spoon touched her lips. Her tongue quivered as her taste buds tingled.

Smiling, Ethan said, "Come on. It's okay."

Emiko reluctantly opened her mouth and accepted the food. Tears materialized in her eyes as she chewed. The food was fine—delicious, in fact. She felt like she was enabling Ethan's erratic behavior, though. She wasn't giving him false hope on purpose, she was just afraid of starving. She had to eat—there were no other options on the table.

Ethan placed the spoon on the tray and said, "You can eat the food by yourself." He chuckled, then he said, "It's probably a little creepy with me feeding you like that. Like I said: I don't want to make you feel uncomfortable. Go ahead and eat. I trust you."

Emiko took a deep breath, then she crawled closer to the tray. She ate the food while constantly glancing up at her captor. She didn't trust him, obviously. Ethan watched with glowing eyes as Emiko devoured the rice and chicken. He didn't mind her lack of manners in the dungeon.

The young man said, "I'm really sorry about what I did earlier. I love you, Emiko. I truly love you. You're the first thing I think about in the morning and the last thing on my mind before bed. You're in my dreams, too. Even when I'm having nightmares, you're there to save me. You're everywhere. I love you so damn much." He stared down at the tray, dejected. He explained, "It's just... I've been stressed lately. It's been a... *frustrating* year for me, for want of a better word. I've been treated poorly in the past, you know? I've been tricked by the succubi before and it's made me do some things I regret."

Mouth full of food, Emiko stopped chewing. She lifted her head from the tray and stared at Ethan with a raised brow.

In an uncertain tone, she repeated, "*Succubi?*"

"Yes, succubi. I'm sure your parents told you about them when you were a child like my mother told me. I don't know, maybe they told you about the incubi, but I'm not sure those even exist. Male demons... It's absurd, isn't it?"

The room became quiet. A droplet of water occasionally plunged from the shower head and plopped on the floor, but the couple did not share another word.

Breaking the silence, Ethan asked, "You don't believe me?"

"I don't know about 'succubi.' Sorry," Emiko responded.

"A succubus is a demon, but it's not like the movies. They look like you or any other woman. They try to seduce men like me to move forward in the world. They don't talk to me because they like me, they just need me to move forward—to climb the ladder of success. Sometimes, they just seduce and torture men for fun. It's sick, but... that's the way life is.

Anyway, I don't think you're a succubus. I think we're having regular 'couple problems.' We can work through it."

Emiko sat, motionless like a stone sculpture. She was awed by her captive's peculiar rambling. She thought: *what the hell is he talking about?* Ethan leaned forward and kissed her forehead. He lifted the tray from the floor as he stood, then he walked towards the doorway.

He said, "Go ahead and get some sleep, sweetheart. I'm going to work a little, then I'll try to get some rest. I'll see you in the morning."

Emiko vacantly stared at the door as Ethan secured the locks. She listened to his every movement. The light under the door vanished with a *clicking* sound. She continued to listen, though. She counted each creaky step on the stairs—*12 steps.* The number wouldn't really help her, but it was something to think about as she wallowed in her misery.

Chapter Thirteen

Couples Fight

Ethan sat at his desk in his bedroom, staring at the blinking cursor on his monitor. The insertion cursor mocked him with each blink, as if it were saying: *you'll never finish this book, they'll never like your writing.* Black bags under his bloodshot eyes, the struggling author felt defeated. He was physically and emotionally drained by the stress.

Dusk had barely arrived, the sun was just falling beyond the horizon, and he already sat in his gray boxer briefs.

He couldn't be bothered to toss on a shirt or some pants. He was solely concerned with his work. *Words, words, words*—he couldn't think of the words to start his new story. He needed to capture his audience's attention with a hook, but his punches were weaker than a toddler's jabs. The page remained blank.

Sunken-eyed, Ethan glanced at the door to his left. He could hear Emiko's persistent screaming. The shouts were faint, the screaming could not be heard from outside, but they were still bothersome. He held his hands over his ears, stomped his feet, and screamed—*frustrated.*

He muttered, "Why won't she shut up? I've treated her right. I've shown her respect. Why won't she let me work, damn it?!"

His chair fell back to the floor as he quickly stood from his seat. He marched out of the bedroom, then he paced back-and-forth—walking between the kitchen and living room.

"Ethan," a man's voice said. "What's going on, champ? Come over here and talk to me."

Ethan whimpered as he dropped his arms to his side. He approached the mirror on the wall. His reflection was talking to him again.

Ethan said, "I'm losing it, man. I can't write my book, Emiko won't stop screaming... It just doesn't feel right. None of this feels right."

"That's because it's *not* right, Ethan," his reflection responded. "You have a big problem on your hands and you know it. You just can't admit it."

"I–I have a... problem?"

"Yes. You have to keep Emiko quiet. If she keeps screaming, someone will find out about her and you'll lose her forever. If that happens... well, *it's over.* You can say goodbye to your career, your lover, and your future. You won't be able to focus on yourself until you can really 'fix' her—until you can trust her. That's your problem."

Ethan nodded, convinced and determined. He was reassured by his own reflection—a creation of his deranged mind.

He stared at himself and whispered, "You're right. She's still not fixed." He glanced over at the basement door and said, "Some discipline and a little scare should fix her, though. Yeah..."

In her room, Emiko shouted, "Help! Somebody help me!"

The young woman stared down at her crotch. The skin was rosy and itchy due to the boiling water. Thick, watery blisters also formed around her vagina. She was afraid to burst the blisters, though. Yet, she couldn't stop scratching. The pain was insufferable.

She screamed, "Call 911! Call someone! Oh, God, I need help!"

Ethan marched down the stairs. He flicked a switch on the wall, which caused the light bulb at the center of the room to illuminate. He tugged on his hair and gritted his teeth as he glared at the door. Emiko's yelling was clearer than ever before—and it infuriated him.

He shoved the door open and barked, "Shut up! Shut your damn mouth!"

From the corner of the room, Emiko sniveled and shouted, "Let me go, bastard! Let me go!"

"Shut up, Emiko! Please... *be quiet.* I've told you several times already: I'll let you go when you're ready. You just–"

"No! Fuck you, you sick bastard! I'm tired of this shit! I'm... I'm tired of everything! I won't stop screaming until you let me go. You hear me, you dirty asshole?! Huh? I *won't* stop screaming until you let me go!"

Ethan tightly closed his eyes and held his hands over his ears. Emiko's screeching drilled into his ears, like the sound of nails scratching a chalkboard— shrill and unnerving.

Emiko glanced up at the ceiling and yelled, "Help! Somebody help me! I'm down here! Please, somebody help me! He's crazy!"

Crazy—the word steamrolled over Ethan. The word was blasphemous in his household. The pain caused by the word was amplified since it came from the woman he loved. A knife was jammed into his back and twisted in his spine, paralyzing him.

Through his gritted teeth, Ethan sternly said, "Don't *ever* call me that again, you filthy cunt."

Emiko stopped screaming and squirmed closer to the wall as Ethan entered the room.

Towering over his captive, Ethan struck down at Emiko with all of his might—left, right, left, right. He repeatedly punched her, landing blows on her head and face—hooks, jabs, uppercuts. Consumed by his rage, he couldn't control himself. He grunted and groaned with each punch. Tears even trickled from his eyes and landed on the back of Emiko's head.

Ethan grabbed a fistful of her hair, then he pulled Emiko's head back—placing the back of her head against the concrete wall behind her. He pulled his leg back, as if he were preparing to punt a football, then he hit Emiko's face with his knee. Emiko was knocked unconscious by the blow to the face. Her head fell to the side.

Ethan stepped in reverse, awed by his own savage attack. He examined his captive's condition as he caught his breath. Emiko's cheeks were red and swollen. A bruise would surely materialize on her left cheek in a day or two. Blood leaked from her nostrils and swollen lips, painting her chin red. A cut formed on the bridge of her nose, too. The black bruise on her temple, which was caused during the night of the kidnapping, appeared to be worsening.

Emiko slowly opened her eyes, as if she were awakening after a peaceful slumber. She frowned as her blurred vision began to focus—she could see Ethan standing over her.

Through her sliced lips, flecked with blood, Emiko weakly said, "You... You're crazy. You're confused... lost... *pathetic.* You don't even know what you're doing. This... This isn't love, it's torture." She giggled deliriously as she shook her head. She said, "You're probably like this because you have a... a little dick. A lot of you are like this because of that... Insecure bastards."

On the verge of breaking down, Ethan nervously chuckled and said, "Little dick... It's always about the cock for you, isn't it? Let me show you something."

Ethan continued laughing as he walked out of the room. Emiko leaned towards her right and stared out of the doorway. She followed the man's every step, watching him with the eyes of a hawk. He reached into the washing machine in the basement. As he glanced back at the room, Emiko returned to the corner—*terrified.*

Ethan stood in the doorway, his right hand hidden behind his back. With a devilish grin on his face, he said, "Let me introduce you to someone. Now, don't get jealous, okay? She's my *ex*-girlfriend and I don't love her. I just use her to... to relieve some stress. Meet Karen, Emiko."

Ethan lifted his right arm and revealed a decapitated head—*Karen's head.* The head was already decomposed. The decomposing head had been reduced to mostly gray skin and bone, although some hair lingered. Maggots and semen filled the head's mouth—Ethan never stopped using it as a fleshlight. Perhaps it was more of a *bone*-light, though. It emitted an atrocious aroma of death, too.

Eyes wide with fear, Emiko stared at the severed head, then at Ethan. She held her hands over her mouth and retched. She struggled to breathe as a lump of anxiety formed in her throat. She was shocked by the revelation.

Ethan walked to the center of the room and shouted, "This is what happens to succubi! Do you want the same thing to happen to you? *Do you?!*"

Sobbing and wheezing, Emiko shook her head and said, "Please don't kill me. I don't want to die. Not like this. Please, don't..."

"You have to prove you're not fake, Emiko. You have to show me you're not a succubus. If you *are* one of them, you'll end up just like Karen. You'll still be with me, but you won't be alive to hurt anyone else. No, you'll only be able to pleasure people. You'll be like her... a *real* fleshlight—but maybe without the flesh. You have to prove yourself."

The room became quiet. Ethan watched his captive with glimmering eyes. Despite the blood and bruises, he was still captivated by her beauty. Emiko kept her head down and eyes low, trying to avoid the decapitated head. She was ready to appease her captor, but she wasn't willing to accept the blood and gore.

Recomposed, Ethan sighed, then he said, "Listen, I'm sorry for hurting you. I'm still frustrated about my book and I couldn't work with your screaming. I couldn't focus without knowing if you were... one of them."

Pretending to apologize, Emiko said, "I'm sorry, too. I didn't know I was bothering you so much. Can you..." She paused to recompose herself, then she asked, "Can you get rid of that thing? *Please?*"

Ethan stared down at the decapitated head, amazed. *It worked,* he thought, *I scared some sense into her.* Like a toy in a child's room, he carelessly tossed the severed head back into the basement. The head bounced on the concrete until it stopped near the cardboard boxes.

Emiko took a deep breath, then she said, "Listen,

I'm... I'm not like the other girls, but I just can't stay here. I'm begging you. Let's go outside. Let's go on a normal date. You don't have to keep me chained up like this. We can be like everyone else. We can be a normal couple."

"I can't let you go like this. It would be like... like releasing a feral animal into the public. We have to wait until you're ready. This is for you as much as it's for me. If I let you go and you're one of *those* things, you'll still end up like Karen. I'm not the only succubus hunter out there, you know? When your love is proven, we'll be free from all of this. I promise."

Emiko's breathing intensified as she fought the urge to cry. She tried to breathe through her nose, but her nostrils were crushed—a snorting sound emerged with each breath. She wiped the tears from her eyes and reluctantly nodded—*okay.* She didn't want to aggravate the situation by challenging him.

Ethan smiled and said, "Good, good. I have a test we can take to... well, to *test* your love."

"A–A test?"

"Yes. It will help me relieve stress and I think it will please you. Hell, we'll even make some money off it. I need to fill my bank anyway. I haven't published anything in months, so my funds are running a bit low. Don't worry, though. I have savings. I can take care of–"

"What are you going to do to me?" Emiko asked, interrupting Ethan's rambling.

"Well, I'm not going to hurt you or anything like that. We're doing this together, okay? Let me just get you something a little more comfortable and sexier to wear. I hope it fits."

As Ethan rushed out of the room, excited like a

child on Christmas Eve, Emiko said, "Wait. Talk to me. What are you going to do?"

The sound of locks *clicking* and *clanking* echoed through the basement. Emiko was left in the room with a storm of wicked thoughts brewing in her mind.

Chapter Fourteen

Webcam

"You like that, don't you, you little slut?" Ethan asked as he thrust into Emiko, savoring the feel of her pussy. He still couldn't believe he was fucking the woman of his dreams. He whispered, "It's amazing."

The couple were having sex on a thin mattress in the main room of the basement, between Emiko's modified bedroom and the laundry machines. Sweat glistening on their bodies, the pair fucked in the doggystyle position—*a classic.* Of course, the sex was not consensual. The rape was also live-streamed on an adult webcam website through Ethan's laptop—and the audience was unaware of the crime.

As he stared at the webcam, Ethan smirked and said, "She likes it. She *loves* it. I know all of you love it, too. I'm back, baby!"

Ethan only wore a black mask with holes on his eyes and mouth. The rest of his muscular figure was presented for the world to see. His face was covered, so he figured he was anonymous.

Against her will, Emiko was given a new outfit for the adult show. She wore a cupless halter bra, revealing her perky breasts, and a crotchless G-string. Her head was covered with a black hood, which also featured a padded blindfold. There was a hole for her mouth, but her mouth was muffled with a large red ball gag. She was handcuffed at the wrists and ankles, too.

As Ethan violently thrust into her, fucking her as if

he had something to prove, Emiko whimpered. She could not speak or scream, she could only cry. The audience couldn't see her tears, though, and her whimpers sounded like moans of pleasure due to the gag. He was not penetrating her too deeply, he was packing four inches after all, but the sex was still painful.

The blisters around her vagina were aggravated with each thrust. Rape was always painful, too.

Emiko wheezed and grunted, struggling to breathe through the mask and gag. Her stomach turned, her heart shattered, and her mind crumbled. She couldn't think clearly. She felt as if her body were invaded by a foreign object. Sex was supposed to be natural, a part of human nature, but it felt surreal to her.

She slumped her head down, planting her forehead on the mattress. She felt numb from head-to-toe—a tingling sensation across her entire body. She could only count the seconds until her captor finished, but each dreadful second felt like a minute. She couldn't whisk herself away from the rape, either.

The racket in the room always brought her back—grunting, moaning, *clanking.* The clanking sound came from the laptop. It was the sound of coins clashing against each other, like the sound of someone winning at a slot machine. The sound emerged each time the audience donated tokens to the couple.

After the show, the tokens could be exchanged for money on the website—one token equaled five cents, and every penny counted. The audience did not approve of rape—most of them didn't, at least. They believed they were watching a sadomasochistic show. They thought it was consensual.

Emiko knew about the audience and the tokens, too. Ethan told her about the website and his plans before setting up the show. The fact made her feel helpless. The world was watching, but no one was helping her. Abandonment was difficult to accept.

Without stopping, Ethan leaned forward and whispered, "Wanna try a different position or are you close to cumming?"

Emiko cried upon hearing the question. The answer was obviously 'no,' but her words were incomprehensible. She couldn't refuse. Saliva dripped from her mouth and mucus soaked her mask as she hysterically sobbed. She could barely breathe, too.

Ethan grabbed her waist, then he flipped her onto her back. He placed his hand around Emiko's neck as she tried to wiggle off the mattress—he wasn't going to let her escape. He pulled her down to the center of the mattress, then he leaned closer to her ear.

He whispered, "Don't do it, Emiko. I'll stop the stream and I'll teach you another lesson if I have to. Don't make me hurt you. Just enjoy the show."

Although she could not see, Emiko turned her cheek to Ethan and looked the other way. A million thoughts ran through her mind, but only one roared over the others: *survive.* Ethan leaned over Emiko's body and stared at the laptop as he continued to thrust. He smirked upon spotting the size of his audience: 1,024 viewers. He glanced at the comments.

A viewer wrote: *Wow, she is so beautiful. Amazing body.*

In Spanish, a user wrote: *Eso llamo una buena chica.*

Another user wrote: *She is gorgeous. Let her ride you, I wanna see her ass.*

Reading a few more comments out loud, Ethan said, "Gorgeous... She's beautiful... She has a great body... Please do more shows with her."

He grinned from ear-to-ear, satisfied with the positive feedback. The compliments were aimed at Emiko, but he took them for himself. Emiko was his lover after all. *I have a beautiful wife,* he thought, *the whole world is jealous.* The smile slowly vanished from his face, reversing into a frown. He narrowed his eyes and tilted his head—confused and offended.

He whispered, "What the hell is this?"

A user commented: *This guy isn't fucking her right. Fucking idiot.*

Another user, a female member according to her profile, wrote: *LOL he's so small! Is that his cock or pinky?* (The message was followed by an emoji with tears of joy.)

An anonymous viewer wrote: *I could fuck your bitch better than you, bro.*

All of the negativity was aimed at Ethan, mocking his size and poor skill. He stared down at Emiko, then at his penis. He became flaccid due to the negative comments, shriveled up like a raisin—about that size, too. He indistinctly muttered to himself, struggling to contain his rage.

Emiko was unaware of the situation. She rested on her back, waiting for the rape to end.

Ethan crawled over Emiko's body and approached the laptop. He jabbed his finger at the webcam and barked, "Fuck you! Fuck all of you! We're giving you a show here! You should be grateful to be able to watch. These little five-cent donations are nothing. You hear me, you cheap, lonely bastards? You should pay us a hundred tokens just to watch! No, *a thousand!*"

Ethan stopped his rant. He hoped he ended the trolling in the chat room through his powerful speech. Unfortunately, nothing could stop an anonymous troll. He only fed them, which only made them stronger.

Another user commented: *Just shut up and fuck her already. Or pay someone else to fuck her and watch from the corner.*

Teary-eyed, Ethan said, "That's what you want, but you won't get it. You wish you could have a woman like her, you wish you were me. You're all wrong, though. You wouldn't be able to love her right. You don't understand the... the *process* of making love. No, you can't have her..."

Tears trickled from his eyes with each blink as he read the comments. The messages were toxic, filled with anonymous hatred. Although a few users offered sympathy, especially towards Emiko, most of the viewers hurled every possible insult at Ethan. He was attacked from every corner. His unusual rants only added fuel to the fire.

Ethan closed the laptop, then he smashed the computer on the floor. A crunching sound echoed through the room. The plastic chipped and scattered across the basement. He swung the laptop at the floor again, which launched more of the plastic across the room. He repeatedly smashed the laptop on the floor.

Between each hit, he said, "She... is... *mine!* I love her! And... and she loves me! You can't have her, damn it!"

Out of breath, he tossed the obliterated laptop aside. He removed his mask, then he glanced over his shoulder and furrowed his brow. During his fit of rage, he didn't notice Emiko had crawled to the corner beside the laundry machine. She glanced every which way, like a drug addict suffering from a bad trip.

Ethan grabbed Emiko's wrists, then he dragged her across the basement. He pulled her into the small room. Despite her resistance, he was able to secure the shackle on her ankle to chain her to the wall. He removed the ball gag from her mouth, then he yanked the hood off her head.

He gazed into her bloodshot eyes and said, "This was a bad idea. I'm sorry, but I... I just can't be around a whore like you—not now. I need some time to think."

He grabbed a set of keys from the floor near the doorway. Emiko watched as he unlocked the handcuffs around her wrists and ankles. He seemed calm, but she could feel the anger brewing inside of him. She couldn't muster the courage to challenge him, though.

As Emiko crawled onto her bed, Ethan walked to the doorway and said, "I can't even look at you right now. I'll... I'll come bring you a fresh set of clothes after I clear my mind. You just... just stay here and think about everything you've done. Good night, Emiko. I... I still love you."

Ethan locked the door behind him, then he departed from the basement. Emiko wrapped the blanket around her body and stared at the door. She tried to stay silent so she wouldn't bother Ethan, but she wasn't strong enough. She snorted and wheezed as she broke down. She couldn't keep her facade afloat. The pain, emotional and physical, was insufferable.

Chapter Fifteen

Crawling Back

Where could an unhinged child grow into a deranged adult? The suburban neighborhood was calm and welcoming. Children screamed and giggled as they played tag on the tree-lined street. A few teenagers strolled down the sidewalks, fiddling with their cell phones. A driver occasionally honked his horn, warning the wandering children. It was noon on a weekend, so the road was busier than usual.

Ethan stood on the sidewalk, his hands on a white picket fence. He gazed at the beige two-story home in front of him—his childhood home. He was struck with a sense of overwhelming nostalgia. The memories, good and bad, brought tears to his eyes. He examined the kempt grass as he walked past the gate. The wood creaked as he strolled onto the porch.

It was all so familiar.

The young man took a deep breath as he stopped at the front door. He had not visited his home since he fell in love with Emiko. He needed a second to prepare himself. *Tap, tap, tap*—he knocked three times, then he sighed.

"I'm coming, I'm coming," a man's voice emerged from behind the door.

Ethan extended his arms away from his body and nervously smiled as the door swung open—*hello.*

John Miller, his father, stood in the doorway. John's curly hair was grizzled. His stubble was hoary, too. He wore a red wool sweatshirt, brown trousers, and brown dress shoes. His style was conservative, but he wasn't a stern man. The big grin on his face was genuine. He was happy to see his son.

John enthusiastically said, "*Ethan!* Where have you been, buddy?"

"Hey, dad. I've just been a little busy lately. I just came over to talk and, you know, I–"

Ethan stopped as a young man approached the door—Corey Miller. Corey was Ethan's sixteen-year-old brother. Wearing black from head-to-toe, he was a moody teenager. He kept his distance from his family, especially when compared to Ethan's close relationship with his mother.

Ethan waved at his brother and stuttered, "H–Hey..."

"Hey, Corey," John said as he patted the youngster's back. He glanced back at Ethan and said, "He was just leaving. He's got a date or something. You know, kid stuff."

"That's good," Ethan responded. He turned his attention to Corey and stuttered, "H–How are you doing, man?"

Corey sighed and shook his head. He wasn't interested in the small reunion. He casually squeezed past his father and his brother.

As he strolled across the walkway, he shouted, "I'll be back at eleven! See ya, Ethan!"

Ethan watched as his estranged brother walked down the sidewalk. He met up with a group of friends one house down. The group bickered and bantered as they walked away. At heart, the lonely author wished he could have had a normal life like Corey.

Breaking his contemplation, John said, "Come in, Ethan. Let's have a little talk."

As he followed his father into the living room, Ethan asked, "Is mom home?"

"No. She's at the store, running errands or wasting my money on some crap. I don't know. She should be back any minute now, though. Take a seat."

John sat on a recliner, Ethan sat on a three-seat sofa. The pair were separated by a glass coffee table at the center of the room. The large flat-screen television didn't capture Ethan's attention, despite his interest in movies. Instead, he examined the family photographs clinging to the walls and sitting on the tables. The pictures depicted a younger version of himself with his baby brother. A few of the pictures showed a seemingly happy couple—John and Brooke. One photograph even depicted John with his cop friends. He was a crime scene cleaner for most of his life.

The pictures allowed him to reminisce about the past. After weeks of uncertainty with Emiko, it felt good to be home.

John asked, "So, what's on your mind?"

"What's on my mind? Well, where do I start?"

"Anywhere. You're here to talk, aren't you? I'm guessing it's something pretty serious if you came here without your mother asking you to come."

Ethan stared down at his reflection on the coffee table. *He can read me like a book,* he thought, *there's no point in lying.*

He said, "You're right. I've been having problems with women lately. I mean, *serious* problems. It's not like high school or college. That's for messing around, for having fun. I can't seem to find the right one, dad. And, when I think I've found her, everything falls apart. I can't tell if it's because of me or her."

John smirked and responded, "Everyone can't be a ladies' man, Ethan. I guess you didn't inherit that from me." He chuckled, then he said, "Don't beat yourself up over the things you've done. I think it's simple. It's the same issue a lot of you young people have nowadays: you're over-thinking this. You need to clear your mind and try to think clearly. Don't think about yesterday or tomorrow, just think about today. Believe me, you'll have many chances to find 'true love' in the future. If you're worried about marriage, *don't*. It means very little nowadays, okay?"

"It means everything to me. Just 'cause it meant nothing to you and mom, that doesn't mean I'm ready to give up on it. I'm not like you and she's not like mom. It won't be the same. She won't have men walking in and out of her bedroom at night while her children watch. I won't fuck hookers all night, then fuck her like nothing ever happened. I won't... I won't..."

John watched as Ethan rambled himself into a corner. His son clearly had more to say, but he couldn't muster the courage to berate his father. The past was shattered, distorted due to forgotten memories. Some secrets were better kept hidden.

John leaned forward and said, "I'm sorry about what you went through as a kid. I never meant to hurt–"

The sound of jingling keys disrupted the apology. The pair glanced over at the front door.

The door swung open and Brooke entered the home, a reusable shopping bag in her arm. She wore a sundress, as she usually did, and her hair was tied in a neat bun. She closed the door with a swing of her hips.

As she strutted across the living room, Brooke said, "Hey, baby. I didn't expect to see you crawling back here so soon. What's going on? You're not asking your father for money, are you?"

"No, mom."

Brooke entered the neighboring kitchen through the archway. She sat her bag on the counter, placed a gallon of milk in the fridge, then she returned to the living room. She fell to the seat beside her son, then she caressed Ethan's hair.

Brooke asked, "You hungry?"

"No."

"Then what do you want?"

"I... I came to talk."

"About what? You don't seem very talkative now. Am I interrupting something between you and your father? Is that it? Am I not good enough to be part of your conversation?"

Elbows on his knees, Ethan leaned forward and dug his fingers into his hair. He was irked by his mother's rotten attitude, but he couldn't challenge her. She positioned herself as the matriarch of the family. He could only sulk and moan.

Chiming-in, John said, "He was just talking about girls. That's all." He muttered, "It's all he ever comes to talk about..."

Wide-eyed, Brooke said, "Oh? Well, tell mommy about your problems. What's wrong, sweetie?"

Ethan sighed, then he said, "It's a long story and I wouldn't want to bore anyone, so I'll just get to the good stuff. I met another woman—a better woman than Karen. I love her, I just don't know if she's 'right.' And, if she's not the one, I don't know what I'm going to do."

"Lock it down."

"Wha–What?"

"You heard me: *lock it down.* If she's better than Karen, better than all of the other trash you've dated, you have to make sure she doesn't get away from you. Marry her, Ethan. You better not let this opportunity slip through your fingers. I'll be *very* angry with you if you do."

Ethan said, "I want to, mom, but it's just–"

"*What?*" Brooke sternly asked.

Ethan grimaced and sniffled, as if he were about to cry. Brooke shook her head and glared at her son, infuriated. John stared down at his lap and sighed, embarrassed. The dysfunctional family was burdened with issues, but they didn't confront them.

Eyes brimming with tears, Ethan said, "I'm... I'm just scared she might be one of the 'bad' ones you used to tell me about. I can't tell anymore."

Brooke explained, "That's fine, Ethan. In fact, that's normal. It's nearly impossible to know which ones are good and which ones are bad these days. They hide behind fake personalities, excessive make-up, and ridiculous cosmetic surgery. Bimbos with bodies like ants... *Christ.* They'll tell you they're real, then they'll stab you in the back. Fortunately, there are some good ones out there and the gamble is worth it. Do you know why?" Ethan shook his head. Brooke continued, "*Babies.* Good or bad, they can all make babies. As soon as you give me grandchildren, *legitimate grandchildren,* you won't have to worry about anything."

Ethan gritted his teeth. He had to fight the urge to kick and scream. He visited his parents in search of reassurance. Instead, he found himself facing his mother's selfish goals while his father passively watched the discussion.

Ethan said, "That's good for *you,* but what about *me?* How will I know if she's good? How will I know if I can truly love her and if she truly loves me?"

"I told you: it doesn't matter."

"*It does.*"

Brooke stared at her son with a deadpan expression. She huffed, then she simpered and shook her head—amused.

With a smug smile on her face, she said, "Believe it or not, the only way to tell for sure is to get married. People show their true colors after they've tied the knot. They feel... comfortable, so they reveal themselves. That's the way society works. You don't find out who you actually love until you're already married. So, *marry her.* Keep her with you and don't let her get away."

Chiming-in, John said, "And, if she rejects you, she probably wasn't the right one to begin with."

"Reject?" Brooke repeated in an uncertain tone. She huffed and rolled her eyes, then she said, "Don't worry about that, Ethan. You don't have to accept rejection. If you want her, *she is yours.* You just have to fix the problem. If she 'rejects' you because you're too big, lose a few pounds; if she dislikes your style, try something new. Whatever you do: don't let her get away. You understand me, right?"

If you want her, she is yours—the sentence stuck out to Ethan. The rest of his mother's advice was insignificant. He heard what he had to hear: justification for his actions. He felt guilty about his treatment of Emiko, he didn't know if his actions were justified. His conscience was dormant, so he used a distorted version of his mother's moral sense to lead him. If the woman said Emiko belonged to him, then he didn't have a problem keeping her by force.

Ethan nodded in agreement and said, "You're right. She's mine and I'm hers. We can work through anything as long as I'm leading her away from the darkness." He smiled as he gazed into his mother's eyes. He said, "I'll think about everything you said. I think I know what I have to do, though. I have to keep her."

Brooke returned the smile and said, "Exactly, darling, exactly..." She caressed his cheek and said, "Your eyes are sparkling. Forget about her for a second. Forget about me, forget about your father... Think about yourself for a moment. Tell me: do you truly love her?"

Again, Ethan stared down at his reflection on the coffee table. The answer was simple: *yes*. As he developed his one-sided relationship with Emiko, he spent most of his time thinking about *her* desires. *Does she love me? Is she a succubus?*–those questions dominated his thoughts for weeks. Succubus or human, mutual or not, he loved her.

And that's all that mattered.

Ethan said, "I love her with all of my heart."

Brooke ran her fingers through his hair and said, "Then that's all you need. It doesn't matter if she's a 'bad' one as long as *you* love her. You make sure she knows that, too. Girls like it when a man takes charge."

"I'll handle it."

"You better. I want grand babies before I'm sixty years old. You might believe otherwise, but I'm not immortal."

Ethan sighed in disappointment. His mother was able to bolster his confidence while burdening his shoulders. As the first-born son, it was his responsibility to bring her a child. At least, that was what he was told since he was a boy.

Brooke said, "We'll come to your place this Sunday for a family dinner so we can finally meet this lover of yours... What did you say her name was?"

"Emiko. Emiko Takahashi."

"Oh, a foreign woman. I'm sure you'll make beautiful babies with her. Until then, remember what we told you."

Ethan stood from his seat and said, "Okay. I'll see you in a few days, I guess. I love you."

"We love you, too," Brooke responded.

John waved and said, "Good luck, champ."

Ethan walked onto the porch and closed the door behind him. He took a deep breath, conflicted by a mishmash of emotions—joy, fear, *anger*. He marched back to his car, determined to fix his relationship before the family dinner.

Chapter Sixteen

Till Death Do Us Part

Ethan leaned on the washing machine, his eyes locked on the door. He watched Emiko's room with narrowed eyes, lost in a labyrinthine mind filled with muddled thoughts. The basement was quiet, but his thoughts were loud. His mind was clouded with doubt, but his heart was pure. He glanced back at his black backpack, which he placed on top of the washing machine.

The backpack was filled with the supplies he needed to achieve his goal. He was prepared to work, but he wasn't emotionally ready to leap forward. *There is no turning back,* he thought, *I won't be able to change her back.* The fact that his actions would be permanent made his decision much more difficult.

Ethan shuddered as he breathed heavily. He tossed his backpack over his shoulder, then he approached the door. His fingers trembled as he turned the keys and unlocked the door. Before he turned the knob, he wiped the sweat from his brow and smiled. He wasn't happy, he just wanted to make Emiko feel comfortable. He pushed the door open and stood in the doorway.

Emiko lifted her head from the blanket. Sleepy-eyed, she gazed at the doorway—blinded by the light in the basement. Upon spotting Ethan's figure, she crawled to the corner and covered her body with the blanket. She was not given a new set of clothes after the failed webcam show. In fact, all of her clothing was removed.

Ethan knelt down in front of her. He appeared ruminative and dejected. He revealed a terrifying range of emotions to Emiko, but he was different. Again, he was impossible to read. He opened his mouth to speak, but he couldn't form a single word. He couldn't even utter a letter. He was rendered speechless by Emiko's beauty—and his horrifying thoughts.

Shivering like a wet dog, Emiko stuttered, "Wha– What are you going to do to me?"

As a tear streamed down his cheek, Ethan asked, "Do you... Do you like it here, Emiko? Do you like my home? Are you comfortable? Are you happy here?"

"Is this a trick question? Are you testing my love? Hmm? Is it a test for... succubi?"

"It's not a test. I just have to know the truth."

Emiko furrowed her brow and tilted her head, baffled. *I hate you, I wish you were dead, I want to leave this disgusting place*—she wanted to hurl every possible insult at him. Words couldn't physically hurt him, words could not stop him. An insult would only bring physical pain to her and she knew that very well.

Emiko said, "I just want to be free. I don't want to be trapped in this room like some animal. I want to leave. I want to see my friends and my family again. I want to hug my brother. I want to kiss my parents... It's not about you, okay? I just need my freedom. That's all."

"I wish I could set you free. I loved watching you at work, school, home... Everywhere you went, you were an absolute angel. I just don't know what to believe."

Emiko crawled forward and seized the

opportunity. She placed her hands on his cheeks and gently stroked his face. She clenched her jaw, fighting the urge to gouge his eyes out.

She said, "You can trust me. I... I love you. Okay? I love you with all of my heart. If you set me free, if you show me you can trust me, I'll love you forever. That's what you want, isn't it? Love? I'm giving it all to you. Please, b–baby, unchain me."

Ethan pulled away from her. He said, "Your love doesn't matter anymore. Everything I said, it was... it was bullshit. I realize that now. I love you and that's all that matters." He grabbed her wrists and pushed her away. Avoiding eye contact, he asked, "Are you feeling okay? Have you felt sick recently?"

Emiko shook her head and asked, "What are you talking about?"

"I noticed some vomit a few days ago. It usually comes with sickness, doesn't it?"

"I... I don't understand. 'It' comes with sickness? Wha–What does?"

Ethan pointed at her stomach and said, "The baby."

Emiko tightly shut her eyes and cocked her head back, as if she were punched by a boxer. An incessant buzzing sound emerged in her ears. She could feel her heart in her throat as sweat trickled across her figure. The revelation hit her like a semi-truck plowing over a deer. The word echoed through her mind: *baby, baby, baby.*

She tossed the blanket aside and stared down at her stomach, awed. She glided her fingertips across her moist belly and nodded. She couldn't deny it anymore. With the light from the basement and her clear mind, she could finally see her baby bump. She wasn't very large, but her belly protruded forward.

An infant of rape was growing inside of her. She felt like an alien was developing in her body.

It wasn't right.

Tears streaming down her cheeks, Emiko stuttered, "B–Baby? I–I'm pregnant?"

Emiko wheezed and wept, shocked. She violently trembled due to an anxiety attack. Ethan couldn't hold a steady face. He grimaced and sniveled. Tears leaked from his eyes and mucus dripped from his nostrils. Hoarse groans escaped his chapped lips as he released his sorrow.

Ethan explained, "I... I did this to you before I brought you here. I went into your apartment and I... I impregnated you. That was almost sixteen weeks ago, Emiko."

"You *raped* me," Emiko sternly responded.

"No, I didn't. I swear, I didn't rape you. I didn't penetrate you like that. Not that time. I... I used a needle and a tube. It was a–a medical procedure. It was professional... You knew you were pregnant this whole time, didn't you? You felt it, right?"

Emiko screamed—a war cry. She swung her arms and kicked her feet as she yelled and cried. Her anger, which she bottled for weeks, burst out of her. She was shocked and disgusted by Ethan's confession. However, at heart, she suspected something had happened. She didn't want to believe it, but she knew it was true. Her screaming changed into a delirious giggle.

In a sense, the situation was ironic.

For weeks, she was accused of being a succubus— and she was beaten and raped due to those accusations. Ethan was the *incubus,* though. He was the evil entity who entered her home as she slept in order to impregnate her. As she giggled, Emiko hammered her stomach with her fists—using her belly as a conga drum. Her goal was simple: *kill the unborn child.*

Ethan grabbed her wrists and pushed her to the wall. He straddled her thighs and tried to stop her. She was determined to abort the pregnancy, though. Ethan pulled his head back, then he slammed his forehead on Emiko's brow—*a skull-rattling headbutt.* He smashed his elbow on Emiko's face, striking her jaw with another vicious hit. With the hit, the woman was knocked unconscious.

Between breaths, Ethan whispered, "I'm sorry. I'm so sorry... After tonight, we'll never fight like this again. Everything's going to change."

***

Emiko rested on her back atop a soft blanket. Her eyelids flickered as she awoke. Her vision was blurred due to a blinding light. She sneered in annoyance, irked by the sudden awakening. She tried to move her arms in order to sit up, but her wrists were shackled. She lifted her head from the blanket and stared down at her feet. Her ankles were shackled, too.

Her limbs were spread away from her body and the shackles were chained to the walls. She could not stand or wiggle away from the center of the room. Halogen lamps on tripods sat at each corner, brightly illuminating the room. Her captor knelt down near the doorway, rummaging through a backpack like a student looking for a pencil.

Emiko stuttered, "Wha–What's going on? What... Oh, no... What are you doing to me, you psycho?!"

Ethan glanced back and smiled. He said, "You're

awake. Good, good. I was starting to worry about you." Still crouching, he turned around and faced his captive. He said, "I went to visit my parents earlier. I spoke to them about our relationship and about love. It was a very insightful conversation. You can learn a lot from your elders. Do you want to know what my mother told me?"

"To–To let me go?"

"Don't be silly, Emiko. She explained love to me— *modern love.* You see, I was obsessing about *old* love. The classical stuff, like *Romeo and Juliet* or... or *Titanic.* That lovey-dovey stuff, you know? My mom gave me a wake-up call, though. She let me know: only *my* love matters. I don't have to be afraid of the succubi anymore."

Emiko shook her head and stuttered, "Wha–What the hell are you saying? What are you going to do to me?"

Ethan sighed as he rubbed the nape of his neck. His mind was swamped, crowded with a million thoughts. He had a lot to explain, but his time was limited. He reached into his pocket, then he pulled out a ring box.

He wagged the box at Emiko and said, "I'm going to fix our relationship, princess. I finally realized what was missing. I found the missing piece, you know? I found hope." His eyes glistened with tears of joy. He said, "Emiko, I'm going to marry you."

Emiko glared at Ethan and said, "You can't just marry anyone you want, you psycho. It doesn't work that way! Damn it, let me go!"

"You're still talking about old love, sweetie. You're talking about that consensual crap. Like I said: only my love matters! You hear me?!"

Ethan deliriously chuckled as he tugged on his moist hair. He was breaking down, crumbling before Emiko's eyes.

He continued, "So, we're going to get married. You're going to have our baby and we'll raise him, *or her,* right. You're probably asking yourself: what's the point of getting married? Well, silly, let me explain it to you. *One:* I think most of our issues stem from a lack of commitment, and marriage will fix that. *Two:* a baby can't be raised without a mother, so you have to stick around. And, *three:* I want everyone to know you belong to *me.* After we're married and as we raise our child, I believe you will *truly* love me. Call me a hopeless romantic, but I'm sure this will work."

With a cracking voice, Emiko said, "Please, don't do this. I just want to go home."

"You're already home and we're going to keep you here forever."

As Emiko sobbed, helpless and hopeless, Ethan opened the box. He showed the ring to Emiko, trying to showcase his dedication. Emiko stared at the ring with sorrowful eyes. Prior to her kidnapping, she had envisioned a beautiful marriage with a wonderful man. Those dreams were destroyed and replaced with nightmares.

The box held a princess-cut diamond wedding ring. The ring sparkled with the bright light.

Ethan said, "I bought this for you. It's beautiful, isn't it? That's 27 diamonds. I had to sell the rights to some of my books to afford this, but... Well, I'd do anything for you." He closed the box, then he returned the case to his pocket. He reached into his bag and said, "Unfortunately, we won't be able to put it on your finger so it will only serve as a *symbol* of our marriage. An expensive symbol, but a symbol nonetheless. You won't be able to wear it when I'm done with you."

Eyes wide with fear, Emiko lifted her head from the blanket and stuttered, "Wha–What? What are you–"

Ethan lunged forward and covered Emiko's face with a moist cloth. Her muffled screams barely seeped past the fabric. She squirmed every which way, trying to escape her captor's grip, but to no avail. The chains restricted her movement. With each passing second, her vision blurred, her heartbeat slowed, and her muscles relaxed.

Ethan leaned closer to her ear and whispered, "It's just a little ether. It won't kill you. It's just so I can work in peace. Don't worry, you won't feel any pain, either. I've got something for you." He reached into his bag and pulled out a needle filled with a clear liquid. He said, "This is a bupivacaine and epinephrine injection. You may have heard of it before. It's usually used by dentists, but this is a little different. It should still have the same effect. It's an anesthetic. You'll need this..."

***

Ethan put a particulate mask over his mouth and nose. He leaned forward, then he injected Emiko's left leg at the upper thigh. He wrapped a belt around the top of her thigh, then he tightly secured it—a makeshift tourniquet.

He rubbed the moist cloth on her face and said, "Everything is going to be fine, darling. When you wake up, everything will be better."

He tossed the cloth aside, then he reached into his bag. He retrieved a hacksaw with a 12-inch blade from his backpack. His eyes watered as he stared at the tool. A diamond couldn't make his eyes glisten like the saw.

He placed the blade under the belt, pushing the teeth into her flesh, then he tugged on the saw. A squishy *crackling* sound emerged as he pushed and pulled on the hacksaw. Blood poured from the grisly gash on her leg, streaming across her thigh and dripping onto the blanket. A few droplets even splattered onto his forearms, shirt, and face.

Yet, the man did not stop sawing into her leg. The exercise required more effort as he sawed deeper into her flesh. The blade jammed every once in a while, forcing him to violently yank and shake the tool. Sweat dripped across his brow as he vigorously sawed through her bone. More blood oozed from the crevice on her leg, spewing like lava from a volcano.

Dazed, Emiko moaned and mumbled, "What... What are you... Don't..."

"Everything is okay, sweetie. It's under control."

He grabbed the moist cloth, then he tossed it over her face. The cloth was bloodied by his hands, but it didn't matter. He continued sawing into Emiko's leg. Squelching, crunching, and groaning echoed through the basement. Blood also squirted from the severed arteries, spraying on the captor like garden sprinklers.

Ethan sighed upon cutting through the entire leg. He pushed the leg aside. The limb was still chained to the wall due to the shackle on her ankle. He grimaced as he stared at her bloody tissue. He had seen it all before, but it still made him uncomfortable. He reached into his backpack and pulled out a gauze roll. He bandaged the wound on her leg with a gauze and left the tourniquet on her thigh.

As he pulled another syringe out of his bag, Ethan smiled and said, "Three more to go, Emiko. After that, you'll be with me forever. Don't worry, I have plenty of anesthesia for the procedure."

Ethan repeated the process three more times. He injected her other leg at the upper thigh, tied a belt around the top of her leg, then he sawed her thigh until he severed the limb. Afterward, he bandaged the wound with a gauze roll in hopes of stopping the excessive bleeding.

The process hardly changed when he moved up to her arms. He injected her upper arm, tied a belt around her shoulder, then he sawed the limb. The wet, crackling sound of flesh tearing and the crunching noise of bones cracking was like music to his ears. The deranged man even bobbed his head and occasionally wagged his finger as he listened to the sounds of death.

Upon severing all of her limbs, Ethan staggered to his feet and sighed in relief. He wiped the sweat from his brow with his forearm, inadvertently smearing blood on his forehead. He unlocked the shackles and grabbed the limbs, then he tossed them into a durable black garbage bag. He walked into the main basement and placed the bag into the washing machine.

He kept all of the fresh human remains in the washing machine until he was ready to dispose of them. He grabbed a towel from the cardboard box, then he wiped the blood off his hands, arms, and face. He couldn't wipe all of it off, though. His clothing was still drenched in blood and his skin remained pink.

He returned to the small room and stopped at the doorway. A lump of anxiety materialized in his throat as he stared at Emiko. The young woman lay on the bloody blanket, limbless. The bandages wrapped around her wounds were soaked in blood. She was freed from her shackles, but she did not appear conscious. Her eyes were closed and her chest and stomach did not rise.

Ethan swiped at his eyes and said, "You're okay, you're okay. You just... You need some rest, right? Everyone needs rest after a significant operation. Everything is fine, right? Yeah, you didn't feel a thing, did you? I did good..."

He smiled and nodded, convincing himself of a fallacy. He knelt down beside her and stroked her hair as he gazed at her face. He kissed her—a gentle kiss on the lips. *A kiss from her prince should wake her,* he thought. To his dismay, Emiko did not awaken. A person could only lose so much blood before they passed away.

The young man caressed her cheek and said, "I'm going to let you sleep, princess. I'll be back to check up on you later. Okay? S–Sleep tight. I... I love you."

Ethan kissed her again, then he exited the room. Despite Emiko's condition, he still locked the door behind him. He held his hands over his face and sobbed as he shambled out of the basement, hoping Emiko would survive the night.

Chapter Seventeen

A Happy Family

The home was deafeningly silent. Floorboards creaked, pipes groaned, and water swirled, but no one spoke. Bloodcurdling shrieks and desperate cries for help did not seep into the living room from the basement. Everyday conversations did not escalate into full-blown domestic disputes. The surrounding world moved at the same pace, conflicted by the same old political and social issues, but the house was different. The couple were abandoned by society, left to fend for themselves.

Ethan sat at the top of the stairs. He stared down into the basement—anxious, curious, frightened. He was unnerved by the silence and flustered by his actions. He didn't feel any guilt when he sawed into Emiko's legs during the previous night. The guilt hit him when he realized he was severely harming his true love. He never planned on pushing her to the brink of death.

He said, "Everything is okay. She's fine. She's just waiting for me to wake her." Strolling down the stairs, he whispered, "I did this for both of us. I did it so you would love me."

Ethan stood in the basement and stared at the door, paralyzed by his fear. The truth waited beyond the barrier, calling his name with a honeyed voice— *Emiko's voice.* He turned the key and opened the locks, then he shoved the door open. The basement light poured into the modified room.

Emiko still lay on her back towards the center of the room. She appeared to be in the same position, too. She didn't move an inch overnight. Blood leaked past the soaked blanket and stained the concrete floor. A rotten stench lingered in the room.

Ethan walked in, then he sat down beside Emiko. He vacantly stared at the wall in front of him, trying to keep his eyes off his captive. He knew she wasn't breathing, but he couldn't face the tragedy. He needed time to heal.

He said, "When I was younger, my mother would always talk to me about girls. She'd tell me about the good girls and... *the succubi.* I liked hearing about the good girls; how they'd stick with me till the end while working so hard to raise our family. I was terrified of the succubi, though. 'They just want your money and your cum,' my mom would say. This was when I was... seven years old." He chuckled and shook his head, then he said, "You're probably wondering if she said those *exact* words to a child. Well, she did. And, she'd even do stuff to me to keep me 'satisfied' until I found the right girl. She didn't want me to get caught up with a succubus, so she'd... she'd do stuff. It–It's hard to explain."

Ethan's breathing intensified as he glanced up at the ceiling. Tears welled in his eyes and his breath broke as he thought about the past. He chuckled again—a nervous laugh to keep a semblance of control.

He continued, "As the years went by, my mother forgot about the good and the bad. She didn't care about me anymore, she only cared about grandchildren. She pushed me to this and there's no turning back. I'm so sorry, princess."

The disturbed man stared at Emiko. He leaned closer and stroked her hair, then he closed his eyes and kissed her. He kept his eyes closed for a moment—*ten seconds*—in order to give her time to awaken. He opened his eyes and frowned.

Kisses could not revive the dead.

Yet, Ethan still refused to accept Emiko's death. *Hibernating,* he thought, *she's just hibernating for the winter.* He crawled down to her legs and gripped her stomach. He squeezed her baby bump as if he were molding a piece of clay.

Ethan said, "We can't lose the baby while you sleep, Emiko. I know, I know. It would devastate the both of us. Besides, I... I promised my mother I would bring her a child. I can't let her down. This is for the baby. *This is for the family.*"

Ethan pulled a boning knife from the back of his waistband. He inhaled deeply, then he thrust the blade into her lower abdomen. Blood spilled from the wound, streaming across her stomach and crotch. He cried as he sawed a horizontal 8-inch incision across her stomach. He pushed and pulled the blade in order to separate her abdominal muscles. *Squelching* and *crunching* sounds echoed through the room during the operation.

He placed the knife on the floor upon loosening the muscles and widening the cut. Using both hands, he dug his fingers into the gash, then he pulled his arms in opposite directions. Through the blood and tissue, he could see the uterus. He held the cut open with one hand and grabbed the knife with the other. He carefully thrust the blade into the uterus. He didn't want to use too much pressure to avoid hurting the fetus. He dragged the blade across the uterus, slicing through the amniotic sac at the same time.

Teary-eyed, he said, "I see you, baby. Daddy's coming."

He gritted his teeth as he cut through the umbilical cord. He tossed the knife aside, then he used both hands to pull the fetus out of Emiko's body. He fell back to his ass, cradling the fetus in his arms like a newborn baby. Through his tearful eyes, he examined his baby.

The infant was the size of an avocado—4-and-a-half inches or so. He could hold the infant in one hand. It already had a humanoid figure—arms, legs, and an erect head. Through the blood, he could see the infant's skin was red and pink. He couldn't tell if the fetus was a boy or a girl, though. Despite the lack of facts, he could make that decision for himself.

He nodded and whispered, "You–You're a girl. You're... You're my princess."

He caressed the fetus' head as he cried. The baby did not breathe, she was clearly dead, but he refused to accept her death. *Like mother, like daughter,* he thought, *she's a heavy sleeper, too.* He held the fetus closer to his chest and swung his arms as he hummed a lullaby. He couldn't help but sob while doing so, too. He instantly fell in love with his daughter.

As he cried, he said, "I can't believe this is happening. Oh, God... I never thought I'd be able to call myself a father. The day is finally here, Emiko. We're parents. We're actually parents." He stared down at the fetus and said, "You need a name. We'll use something from mommy *and* daddy, okay? Don't worry, I did some research. We'll call you Mirai— *Mirai Miller.* I read Mirai means 'future' in Japanese. You're our future, princess. You're everything to me."

Drenched in blood, Ethan staggered into the basement with the tiny fetus cradled in his arms. He placed his cell phone on the laundry machine, then he flicked his finger across the screen. A love song played through the speakers. He sashayed in the center of the room, swinging his hips and shaking his shoulders. He danced with Mirai—a father-daughter dance.

He placed his chin on her head and whispered, "I love you, princess. You mean everything to me. I can't wait to watch you grow up. I'm going to give you the world. Your mother's going to lose her mind when she wakes up and sees you." He chuckled, then he kissed her bloody forehead. As he swayed left-and-right, moving with the music, Ethan whispered, "Your mother and I... We'll love you forever, princess."

Blood on his arms, face, and clothing, the young man continued to dance with his deceased child. Tears of joy trickled from his eyes as he thought about the future. The dungeon was grim, death plagued his home, but he saw a brighter tomorrow.

Ethan and Mirai, they danced the night away...

Chapter Eighteen

The Family Dinner

The scent of mashed potatoes, gravy, and ham drifted through the home. Water for coffee and tea boiled in a kettle on the stove. Plates, Silverware, and folded napkins were set on the table for five people. Ethan dipped his fingers into the mashed potatoes, then he tasted the dish. He dipped his finger into the homemade gravy, then he tasted the sauce.

He smirked and said, "It's perfect. It's all perfect." As he fiddled with the knobs on the stove, he said, "My parents can be a little strange, but I think everything will be fine. I mean, whose parents aren't strange, right? I'm sure your parents are a little 'off,' too. My mom is strict but caring. Don't take it personal if she runs her mouth a bit. My father did some bad things in the past, but he's okay these days. He's not so strict, you know? My brother... I hardly know my brother. I don't know why, but we just never connected."

He wiped his hands on his white bib apron and turned around. He smiled as he stared at the rectangular table—three seats on the long sides, one at each end.

Emiko's body was poised on the first seat to the left, a pillow placed under the small of her back. The gash on her stomach was crudely sewn shut. Her other wounds were properly bandaged, but blood still dripped from her chair and plopped on the floor. Her face was still swollen and bruised, too. Her sleeveless black dress reached down below her severed legs.

Mirai sat on a highchair beside her mother. Due to her puny size, she could not reach the chair's tray. She was slumped back in the seat, limp and lifeless. She wasn't wearing any clothes, either. Ethan couldn't find anything that would fit. Her fragile body was clean, though. She was still pink, but the blood was gone.

Ethan grabbed a towel from the counter. He knelt down under the table and cleaned the blood from the floor.

As he scrubbed, the troubled writer said, "There's nothing to be embarrassed about, Emiko. Hey, women bleed once a month, right? If they ask, we'll just tell them you're on your period. No big deal."

He stood and tossed the towel on the counter. He spit on his hands, then he ran his fingers across Emiko's tousled hair. He tried to fix her hair to the best of his ability, but it still remained disheveled. He liked it, though.

He kissed her forehead, then he asked, "Are you ready to meet the family?"

Emiko did not respond. She sat on the seat, a vacant stare on her face. Ethan nervously chuckled as he patted her shoulder, trying to persuade her to talk. On the verge of breaking down, he grimaced and wheezed.

"I'm ready, sweetie," a feminine voice emerged from the back of his head.

Ethan cracked a smile—he recognized the voice. Although her lips did not move, Emiko's voice still remained in his head. It was enough to boost his confidence. He sighed in relief. He kissed Emiko's brow again, then he kissed the top of Mirai's head.

In a soft voice, he said, "They're going to love you, too, Mirai. Grandma is going to go crazy when she sees you."

He kissed the top of her head again, then he rubbed her tiny dome—as if he were petting a dog. He returned to the stove and checked on the gravy. Despite the dead bodies sitting at the kitchen table, he continued his day as if nothing were wrong.

He said, "This is the first step towards our future. You just have to meet my family, they have to accept you, then we move on to the next step. Of course, that means I have to meet your family, too. I know your family might not like me, but we have a kid now. They have to accept me. If they don't... Well, we'll always have my family. We wouldn't want their negative energy anyway. We're on the right path, sweetie. Believe me, this is–" The doorbell echoed through the home. Ethan glanced over his shoulder and whispered, "They're here..."

***

Ethan wiped his clammy palms on the towel, then he removed his bib apron. He smiled and nodded at Emiko and Mirai, trying to keep a semblance of control in front of his deceased family. He marched across the living room, then he stopped at the front door. *A second*—he only needed a second to mentally prepare himself.

Grinning from ear-to-ear, he opened the door and said, "It's good to see you. You all look great."

"Of course we do," Brooke responded, wearing a black knit dress with a bulky coat draped over her shoulders. "What did you expect? We're about to meet the future 'Mrs. Miller.' We can't show up looking like trash and setting a bad first impression."

Ethan laughed and nodded—*sure, sure.* He glanced over at his father. John wore a white button-up shirt with a red tie, black trousers, and matching dress shoes. He cleaned up nicely. He held a brown bag in his right hand.

With a big grin on his face, he held the bag up and said, "I brought some nice wine and chocolate for your lover. I'm very excited to meet this fine young woman. Jeez, I feel like I'm dating again."

Brooke rolled her eyes and said, "Of course you do. You bought wine and chocolate for all of your old whores back then, too, didn't you?"

The group became silent—an awkward silence. Brooke stood with her arms crossed as she tapped her foot while John lowered the bag and shrugged.

Ethan said, "Anyway, um... Come in, come in. Dinner is almost ready."

Ethan watched as his parents walked into his home, wiping their feet on the doormat before stepping foot in the house. His eyes widened upon spotting a third visitor on his porch—Corey Miller.

His brother, dressed in all black as usual, fiddled with his cell phone on the porch. The young man was not dressed in formal attire and he didn't appear interested in the family dinner. He showed up, though, and that was enough to warm Ethan's heart.

Awed, Ethan said, "Corey, you're here..."

Corey glanced up at Ethan, then he huffed—*whatever.* He walked through the doorway without sharing a word with his older brother. The youngster took a gander around the living room as he walked towards the kitchen.

As Corey explored, Brooke and John stood near the

front door and looked at the family pictures clinging to the walls. They beckoned to Ethan, inviting him to reminisce about the past. The family huddled in front of the pictures and told stories about each photo. Most of the photos depicted a happy family.

In reality, the family had been broken and distant since Ethan was born. A picture could tell a million lies.

Corey sneered in disgust and pinched his nose as he walked through the living room. The putrid stench of death pummeled his nostrils. He stopped in the archway, one foot in the kitchen and the other in the living room—*frozen.* He clenched his jaw and swallowed loudly as he stared at the dead bodies sitting at the kitchen table as if everything were normal. He sighed and shook his head.

He glanced over his shoulder and shouted, "Mom! He did it again!"

Near the front door, Brooke furrowed her brow and asked, "Did what?" She glanced at Ethan and asked, "What did you do this time, boy?"

"I–I just did what you told me. I... I did what you told me to do."

"What the *hell* did you do, Ethan?"

As Ethan indistinctly stammered, Brooke jostled her way past her son. John frowned and followed his wife. The family stood in the kitchen archway. Father, mother, and son shared grimaces of disgust. They did not appear surprised, though. They didn't gag or cry, they were just appalled and disappointed.

John shook his head and said, "Goddammit. I thought it was different this time, Ethan. I thought it was real. Look at the mess you've made, boy. You cut her and you..." His eyes widened upon catching a glimpse of the fetus. Shocked, he turned towards his son and asked, "Did you take the damn baby out by yourself?"

Ethan stuttered, "I–I *saved* the baby, dad. Her name is Mirai. It means 'future' in Japanese. I saved her to–to save my future. Everything is okay, though. It all worked out... right?"

John frowned and shook his head, disappointed. He walked around the kitchen table and examined the bodies.

He said, "Shit, they're really dead. They must have died recently, too. I bought this expensive wine for nothing."

"Well, you can use it to get shit-faced while you clean up his mess," Brooke suggested.

"You want me to clean this? *Again?* This is a lot of work, Brooke. He needs to start taking responsibility for his actions. He needs to learn how to clean his messes by himself."

Brooke sternly said, "You're going to clean it up. What else are you good for, John? Hmm? You're a has-been crime scene cleaner. You don't have a job anymore and your 'specialty' is useless around the house since you don't clean. The least you can do is clean up your son's mess."

John sighed, irked. He had been cleaning Ethan's messes for years, disposing dead bodies, cleaning forensic evidence, and fixing his son's mistakes. He even helped him get rid of Karen's torso. He glanced over at Ethan. He considered leaving his son with the mess, but he couldn't abandon his family. He couldn't go against the matriarch, either. Yet again, he decided to use his skills to clean his son's mess.

As John reached for Emiko's body, Ethan lurched

into the kitchen, shoving his way past his mother and brother. He slid to a stop at the table and held his arm between his father and his lover.

Teary-eyed, he asked, "What are you doing?"

John said, "She's dead, Ethan. You can't keep her in your home, so I'm going to get rid of her. Are all of her belongings in the basement."

"Y–Yes... I have some... some pictures of her in my room, too. But you don't have to–"

"I'll get to that later. You'll probably need some new computers. Don't worry, I'll take care of it."

Ethan grabbed his father's wrist and said, "No, no, no. Please, don't do this. She's okay, dad. She's fine. I mean, if she looks sick, we can just take her to the hospital, right? *Right?*"

John stared at his son with a set of disappointed eyes. He was genuinely hurt by his son's mental condition and his lack of aid. He could clean Ethan's mess, but he couldn't cleanse his mind—and that fact hurt him. Being a helpless parent was painful.

He said, "No. Go to your mother. I'll take care of this."

Ethan reluctantly released his father's wrist and stepped aside. He stepped in reverse until he bumped into his mother. His eyes welled with tears as he watched his father. The man lifted Emiko's torso off the chair, then he lugged her into the basement—grunting and groaning with each step. Emiko was petite, but her lifeless body was heavy.

Corey muttered, "I told you this was going to happen." He sighed, then he said, "I'm leaving. Alright, mom? I'll be home by midnight."

Brooke casually waved and said, "Go on. Stay out of trouble."

Corey took one final glance at Ethan. He could see his brother was sad and confused, but he couldn't muster a shred of sympathy. His older brother was a psychotic serial killer who frequently tortured and killed innocent people. Family protected family, but the idea could only go so far. He sighed and walked away, leaving his brother to wallow in his sorrow.

Brooke approached the table. She puckered her lips and shook her head as she stared at the fetus. *So close,* she thought, *we were so damn close.* She grabbed the nape of Mirai's neck with her fingertips and lifted her from the highchair. With her arm extended forward, away from her body as if she were carrying a soiled diaper, she approached the basement door.

Ethan asked, "She's dead, too?"

Brooke nodded and said, "Yes. Darling, go to the living room and lie down. I'll come talk to you in a bit." Ethan held his hands over his mouth and sobbed. Brooke smiled and said, "Everything's going to be okay, sweetie. Don't worry about it. I'll take good care of her, okay? Go on. Give me a minute with your father."

Ethan gazed at his daughter, trying to memorize every nook and cranny on her figure. Heartbroken, he reluctantly followed his mother's directions.

He shambled into the living room and mumbled, "I love you, Mirai. I'm sorry for everything I did."

As her son left her sight, Brooke leaned into the basement and said, "Get rid of this one, too, John."

She nonchalantly tossed the fetus down the stairs, causing the infant to roll to the bottom of the steps. Sneering in disgust, she vigorously washed her hands in the sink. She breathed deeply, as if she were preparing for a performance, then she strutted to the living room with a fake smile plastered on her face.

***

In the fetal position, Ethan lay on the sofa with his head on his mother's lap. Tears trickling from his eyes, he held his hands to his face and stared at the television across the room. He didn't care about the news. It was all sociopolitical manufactured bullshit to him. He was lost in his thoughts, pondering the consequences of his actions.

He thought: *was it really my fault? Did I kill Emiko and Mirai?*

Without taking his eyes off the television, he sniffled and asked, "What happened, mom?"

Brooke clicked her tongue and *awwed* upon hearing the question. She stroked her son's hair, coddling him as if he were an infant.

She explained, "I know it's hard to accept, baby, but what's done is done. Your little girlfriend is dead and the baby did *not* survive. That's the truth. You have to accept it."

Ethan panted as he processed the news. He buried his face into his mother's thighs and bellowed. He kicked his feet and swung his arms as he indistinctly mumbled. He had hoped, by some miracle, the news would change.

Brooke said, "Calm down, darling, calm down. You can cry all you want, but it's not going to bring them back. It's your fault anyway, Ethan. *You* killed them. You should know all of this by now."

"I... I didn't mean to hurt them. I was... I was just doing what *you* told me to do. You said to make her mine so I did. I didn't want to kill them. They weren't supposed to die."

"Your father was right. You need to stop blaming everyone else for your actions. Stop acting like such a child," Brooke scolded. Ethan remained silent for ten seconds, then he burst into tears. Brooke sighed, then she said, "Okay, okay. I guess I'm not really helping, am I? Maybe I had *some* hand in this, too. I can share some of the blame."

Although he still felt a stinging pain in his heart, some of the burden was lifted from his shoulders. He felt some relief thanks to his mother's admission of guilt, despite her reluctance to self-incriminate. He continued to whimper and moan as he stared at the television.

Brooke said, "I should have been around more often—then and now. I should have raised you better and I should have met this woman days ago. I guess I pushed you a little too hard, didn't I? Well, I'm sorry about that."

"I'm sorry, too. It was my fault."

The pair shared a moment of silence, accepting the apologies without uttering another word. *Crunching* and *popping* sounds echoed from the basement as John cut into Emiko's body, but the afternoon was relatively tranquil.

Breaking the silence, Ethan said, "I'm scared, mom. I feel so alone, like I've been abandoned by everyone. I'm afraid I'll never find true love without Emiko. God, I loved her so much."

"There are plenty of fish in the sea, Ethan."

"But there was only one Emiko."

"Believe me, you'll find someone better. You just have to keep your eyes open. You're an amazing boy, Ethan, and someone's going to be very lucky when they meet you," Brooke said. She glanced over at the basement door, concerned. She said, "You have to stay free, though. This is going to be just like those other times, darling. The police are going to ask questions... if they haven't already."

"They haven't."

"Good. You know the drill, right?"

Ethan sighed and nodded, disappointed. He had been in the same situation before. His father could clean a crime scene, but he couldn't erase memories. Witnesses, like Burt and Charles, would surely link him to Emiko's disappearance.

Brooke asked, "What do you say if the police ask you any questions?"

"*Nothing*," Ethan responded. "I say nothing. I invoke my right to remain silent. I ask for a lawyer if they want to ask questions and I ask for a warrant if they want to look around. Regardless, I *never* answer any of their questions."

"That's very good. You know, most people end up in prison because they self-incriminate themselves. Prosecutors, detectives... They'll twist your words, even if you did nothing wrong. It's better for you to remain quiet the entire time. That is, if anything happens at all."

Ethan asked, "Did I do something wrong?"

"It depends on who you ask. I think you're just misunderstood. Try not to think about it too much. We're cleaning everything up. As soon as we push through this, you can move on and start looking for a new mate. Then, you can bring me my first grand-baby."

Ethan vacantly stared at the wall above the television. He thought about Emiko's death, he brooded over Mirai's unfortunate passing. He couldn't see a bright future, but there was a glimmer of hope in the darkness. *I'll find someone who understands me,* he thought, *even if it takes me until the day I die.* He was disheartened, but he would survive.

Chapter Nineteen

Love Never Dies

Ethan sat by his lonesome at the corner booth of a small diner. The scent of pungent coffee and fresh baked goods drifted across the eatery. A few people sat at the bar, bickering about the football game on the television, while some families enjoyed a freshly cooked breakfast at the other booths and tables. A few waiters and waitresses walked around, happily serving their patrons.

The young author shoved some scrambled eggs into his mouth, then he took a sip of his coffee. He kept his head down and avoided eye contact, trying to keep a low profile. The manager and employees didn't know him, he rarely visited the diner, but he still tried his best to lay low. Four weeks had passed since Emiko's death, but he still couldn't get over her.

"This place was really hard to find," a male voice said from beside the booth.

Ethan glanced to his left—he could only see the man's black pants and polished dress shoes. He slowly lifted his head, examining his two-button coat, crisp white button-up shirt, and expensive tie. He recognized the man's golden locks, crystal blue eyes, and chiseled face. His agent, Paul Davis, stood beside him.

Paul asked, "Do you mind if I sit down?"

"Go ahead."

Paul took a seat across from Ethan. Elbows on the table, he clasped his hands in front of him and gazed at his client. Ethan furrowed his brow and leaned back, baffled by the awkward stare. He couldn't tell if he had good news or bad news for him.

Ethan asked, "What is it?"

Paul grinned and said, "You did it, Ethan. I finished reading through your manuscript and... *you did it.* We have a hit on our hands. This new horror book you wrote... It's exactly what we needed. It's a raw, disturbing, and emotional look into the lonely psychopath's mind. It's violent, it's gruesome... It's controversial, and controversy sells. Psychos are going to be lining up to purchase this."

"They're not psychos."

Paul cocked his head back and responded, "Excuse me?"

"The readers are not psychos. They just like the darker side of things. They enjoy the macabre like everyone else, they're just not afraid to admit it. Besides, I don't think you'd know a psycho if he sat across from you and looked you in the eye."

Paul nodded and said, "I suppose you're right. Either way, there's an audience out there waiting to read something like this. I mean, it's just so... I don't even know how to explain it. How'd you come up with such a vicious idea?"

How do you come up with your ideas?–many authors were not fond of the question, but it was very common. The young writer sighed as he rubbed the nape of his neck. He could tell the truth—*it was inspired by a woman I kidnapped and killed*—or he could lie. The choice was obvious.

Ethan said, "It came to me in a dream. Just like the book, it was about a confused man who kidnapped a woman in order to fall in love and make a family. I just... I kept seeing this woman chained up like an animal in a basement. I had to write about it. I had to preserve it."

Wide-eyed, Paul said, "Jesus, Ethan, it sounds more like a nightmare to me."

Ethan shook his head, shrugging off the poignant memories. He asked, "Will anything have to be censored? Was it too violent?"

"I don't know, but I'm going to try to push the version you gave me. The people are going to want the director's cut, not the pussy's cut."

Ethan frowned and stared down at his coffee. He didn't care for the crass conversation, but he couldn't muster the courage to end it.

Paul continued, "We're going to make a lot of money off this book. I'm going to start contacting a few more publishers so we can start selling the rights worldwide. Listen, we're going to push so many more units if we can get this translated to German. They love these types of stories over there. I'm telling you, I think we hit a gold mine. I won't have to hound you to write another book for months."

"Good, good."

Paul raised his brow and shrugged. He was selling dreams with his words, but Ethan appeared to be trapped in a nightmare. He expected Ethan to clap and hug him. The author, however, remained indifferent.

Paul asked, "Are you okay, Ethan? I thought you'd be celebrating. You could have a *real* hit on your hands."

"I'm fine. I'm just thinking about the next book," Ethan responded.

"You should be thinking about taking a vacation.

You deserve it, man."

"Thanks for the suggestion, but I just want to stay busy."

Paul puckered his lips and nodded. Knowing he wouldn't be able to convince him otherwise, he withdrew from the conversation.

The agent said, "Alright, well, I'll call you when everything's settled. Enjoy your day, Ethan. Take care of yourself."

"You too."

Ethan leaned on the window and stared at the busy street as Paul departed from the diner. People walked on the sidewalks and rushed across the crosswalks while drivers zoomed down the streets. The women were beautiful, but he was not aroused. He didn't feel any magic with the strangers—a spark did not ignite his love.

Depressed and exhausted, he imagined throwing himself in front of a semi-truck. It would be a bloody spectacle. Besides, suicide seemed like an appropriate ending to his story.

"Excuse me, sir," a woman said from beside the booth.

For the first time in weeks, Ethan glanced up and made eye contact with a stranger. He found himself staring at a young brunette woman. The waitress wore a blue A-line dress under a white waist apron— an old-fashioned uniform. The quaint uniform was attractive. She had a sexy figure, too—*curvy.* Her dark brown eyes in particular caught the author's attention.

The young woman asked, "Will you be having anything else?"

Stunned by her beauty, Ethan stuttered, "Wa–

Wasn't someone else serving me? A–A man?"

"Yeah, sorry about that. He had to run out for a minute and I couldn't just leave you waiting here. Do you want the check or would you like some dessert?"

"I–I'll have the apple pie."

"Okay. I'll be right back with that."

Ethan watched as the waitress strolled into the kitchen. He didn't leer at her ass or ogle her legs. He stared at the back of her head, hoping to catch another glimpse of her eyes. He could feel the butterflies swarming in his stomach. He could feel the magic.

The waitress returned to the booth. She smiled and nodded at Ethan as she placed a plate on the table. She wasn't giving him any special treatment. She treated him like every other customer—but her kindness was misconstrued.

The woman said, "Feel free to call me over if you need anything else."

Before she could leave, Ethan grabbed her wrist and pulled her back to the booth. As the couple locked eyes, he nervously smiled and asked, "What's your name?"

Join the mailing list!

Enjoy the book? Want more revolting, *uncompromising* horror? Well, I release disturbing horror books on a monthly basis. You can sign-up for my mailing list and I'll let you know when the next book is available. Don't worry, either, I won't stalk you or anything like that. This book wasn't inspired by me, I swear. Anyway, by joining my mailing list, you'll be the first to know about new releases, deep discounts, and free books. Best of all, it requires very little effort on your part—and it's free! Oh, and you'll only receive 1-2 emails per month. Visit this link to sign-up: http://eepurl.com/bNl1CP

Dear Reader,

Hello! Thanks for reading *Erotomaniac.* This was a little different from my usual. I usually write books about extremely violent serial killers. I think this book was *a little* less violent and it was obviously focused on a stalker, who happened to be a serial killer. It's different, right? Still, it was pretty disturbing. I even had trouble writing the gory climax. So, someone out there might be offended. If you stumbled upon this book and ignored the warnings, please understand: it was never my intention to offend.

Erotomaniac was inspired by two things: classic stalker movies, like *One Hour Photo*, and erotomania. Erotomania is defined as an excessive sexual desire or a delusion where a person believes *another* person is in love with them; those suffering from erotomania may also believe that their 'lover' is communicating with them through telepathy. Ethan is the person suffering from erotomania in this case. He's also a violent serial killer who murders his girlfriends when he believes they are succubi—he's a maniac. So, yeah, I combined erotomania and maniac for the title and the premise of this book. That was my inspiration.

I tried to make this as creepy as possible by putting myself in the shoes of a stalker. The shoes didn't quite fit me, I don't have a knack for stalking, but I think I created a creepy experience.

I used real stories of stalking and modified them. Sometimes I even thought: *what would I do if I were stalking her?* It wasn't the best mind frame, but it really helped me delve into the mind of a lonely stalker. Well, the lonely part was easy since I *am* lonely, you know, but... I digress.

Just to be clear: I *don't* condone the act of stalking. I write these type of *human* horror stories because they feel *real,* not because I think they're 'cool.' Stalking is also a crime and crime is interesting to me. For those of you who don't know, I'm a *Criminal Justice* graduate and I've always been interested in *Criminology*, so I'm drawn to the dark side of the human mind. Also, here's something to think about: this could be happening to you. Someone could be looking at your Facebook photos and doing the same as Ethan. It's an eerie idea, isn't it?

Anyway, if you enjoyed this book, *please* leave an honest review on Amazon.com. Your review is *very* important to me. In fact, my entire career *depends* on your review. Your review helps me improve on future books and it helps other readers find this book. In turn, the more readers I attract, the more I can write. So, if you liked this book, a review will help me release more—and it'll only take five or so minutes. This book is categorized as an 'extreme horror' book. Was it extreme enough? Was it too dark and disturbing? Did you like the focus on characters? Was it too personal and real? Or was it not authentic enough? Would you like to read another stalker story by me in the future? Answering questions like these will allow me to better understand you, the reader. Your words have the power to influence my writing—please use them wisely.

Also, feel free to share this book with your friends and family. Tweet it to your followers on Twitter, share it with your friends and family on Facebook, lend it to them, or even read it to them over the phone or video chat. Birthday, holiday, or special event coming up? Buy them a copy as a gift. Word-of-mouth is a superb method in supporting independent authors—and it's mostly *free.*

Your support has helped me immensely. Although I could be cutting corners and spending my earnings on myself, most of the money I make off my books is *reinvested* into my books. I get better covers, I spend on marketing, and so on. So, yeah, I'm still poor.

Finally, if you enjoy scary stories, feel free to visit my Amazon's Author page. I've published over a dozen horror novels as well as some science-fiction/fantasy books. If you're looking for more disturbing horror, check out *Mason's Television.* If you'd like to read a psychological horror book, check out my next release, *Madness at Madison Mall*—it should be out in June 2017. Please keep your eyes peeled for my upcoming books since I release a new book every month.

Feel free to check out my older novels in the meantime. I really appreciate it! Once again, thank you for reading. Your readership keeps me going through the darkest times!

Until our next venture into the dark and disturbing,
Jon Athan

P.S. If you have questions (or insults), you'll receive the quickest and most efficient response via Twitter @Jonny_Athan. If you're an aspiring author, I'm always happy to lend a helping hand. I know how difficult it can be to get started, so feel free to ask. You can also like my Facebook page and talk to me there. And, I also have a business email which you can use to contact me: info@jon-athan.com. Thanks again!

Printed in Great Britain
by Amazon

54221710R00102